'A tender, earnest first novel . . . Van Booy wisely resists romanticizing torment, instead suggesting that grief – tied as it is to fate and faith – can give way to promise.' *Publishers Weekly*

'A swift and engaging story.' *Wall Street Journal*

'His prose is music, and his characters are warm-hearted, gentle, bemused, philosophical beings . . . It's as if Shakespeare's Sonnet No. 30 has unfolded into a full-blown novel.'
East Hampton Star

'Van Booy's writing rings with the proverbial pithiness of Oscar Wilde, the elegance of F. Scott Fitzgerald, the clarity of Graham Greene and the wit of Evelyn Waugh, conjuring a strong voice full of poetic, timeless grace.' *San Francisco Examiner*

'Van Booy's writing seduces from the first page . . . He is a hugely gifted writer.' *Portland Press Herald*

'The exquisite prose and heartbreaking (but never hopeless) emotional honesty make it a worthy read.' *Daily Candy*

Love Begins in Winter

'Simon Van Booy knows a great deal about the complex longings of the human heart, and he articulates those truths in his stories with pitch-perfect elegance. *Love Begins in Winter* is a splendid collection, and Van Booy is now a writer on my must-always-read list.'
Robert Olen Butler, author of *Severance* and *A Good Scent from a Strange Mountain*

'Simon Van Booy seems to start with a story in mind and then to turn it into a poem without losing its narrative power. *Love Begins in Winter* is an exquisite show of force.'
Roger Rosenblatt, author of *Lapham Rising* and *Beet*

‘*Love Begins in Winter* brings to life the wistfulness of youth and the possibilities of young love with clear and graceful prose.’

Jamie Saul, author of *Light of Day*

‘The stories of *Love Begins in Winter* are stylistically brilliant and emotionally beautiful. I found myself gasping, literally gasping, at surprises so perfectly attuned as to be inevitable. Simon Van Booy is an extraordinary writer, and this is a book to be read and reread again and again.’

Binnie Kirshenbaum, author of *The Scenic Route*

‘Beautiful . . . each of these stories has moments of sheer loveliness.’ *Publishers Weekly*

‘Pitch-perfect . . . Convincingly shows how love rights the world.’ *Kirkus Reviews*

The Secret Lives of People in Love

‘These tales have at once the solemnity of myth and the off-handedness of happenstance.’ *Publishers Weekly*

‘[Van Booy] shows an uncanny ability to create intense moods and emotions within the space of a few poetic paragraphs.’

Booklist

‘Lovely and genuinely touching. This talented author bears watching.’ *Kirkus Reviews*

‘Breathtaking . . . chillingly beautiful, like postcards from Eden . . . Van Booy’s stories are somehow like paintings the characters walk out of, and keep walking.’ *Los Angeles Times*

To Luke and Christina

ALSO BY SIMON VAN BOOY

FICTION

Everything Beautiful Began After

Love Begins in Winter

The Secret Lives of People in Love

EDITED EDITIONS

Why We Fight

Why We Need Love

Why Our Decisions Don't Matter

The Illusion *of* Separateness

Simon
Van Booy

ONEWORLD

A Oneworld Book

First published in Great Britain by Oneworld Publications 2013
This paperback edition published by Oneworld Publications 2014
Reprinted 2015

Published by arrangement with HarperCollins Publishers, New York, New York, U.S.A

A CIP record for this title is available from the British Library

ISBN 978-1-78074-394-3
ISBN 978-1-78074-325-7 (eBook)

Designed by William Ruoto
Printed and bound in Denmark by Nørhaven A/S

This is a work of fiction. While, as in all fiction, the literary perceptions and insights are based on experience, all names, characters, places, and incidents either are products of the author's imagination or are used fictitiously.

Oneworld Publications
10 Bloomsbury Street
London WC1B 3SR
England
www.oneworld-publications.com

We are here to awaken from the illusion
of our separateness.

– THICH NHAT HANH

MARTIN

LOS ANGELES,

2010

I.

THE MERE THOUGHT of him brought comfort. They believed he could do anything, and that he protected them.

He listened to their troubles without speaking.

He performed his duties when they were asleep, when he could think about his life the way a child stands in front of the sea. Always rising at first light, he filled his bucket, then swished along the corridors with pine soap and hot water. There were calluses where he gripped the handle. The bucket was blue and difficult to carry when full. The water got dirty quickly, but it didn't annoy him. When it was done, he leaned his mop against the wall and went into the garden.

He sometimes drove to the pier at Santa Monica. It was something he did alone.

A long time ago, he proposed to a woman there.

There was mist because it was early and their lives were being forged around them. They could hear waves chopping but saw nothing.

In those days, Martin was a baker at the Café Parisienne. He had a moustache and woke up very early.

She was an actress who came in for coffee one morning and never quite managed to leave.

She would have liked the Starlight Retirement Home. Many of the residents were in films. They come to breakfast in robes with their initials on the pocket. They call him *Monsieur* Martin on account of his French accent. After dinner they sit around a piano and remember their lives. They knew the same people but have different stories. The frequency with which a resident receives guests is a measure of status.

Martin is often mistaken for a resident himself.

It would be easier if people knew exactly how old he was, but the conditions of his birth are a mystery.

He grew up in Paris. His parents ran a bakery and they lived upstairs in three rooms.

When Martin was old enough to begin school, his parents seated him at the kitchen table with a glass of milk, and told him the story of when someone gave them a baby.

'It was summer,' his mother said. 'The war was on. I can't even remember what the man looked like, but there was suddenly a child in my arms. It happened so quickly.'

Martin liked the story and wanted to know more.

'Then she brought the child into my bakery for something to eat,' his father said.

'That's right,' his mother added. 'It's how we met.'

His father stood at the dark window and confessed to the reflection of his son how they waited years before doing anything official.

His mother's tears made circles on the tablecloth. Martin looked at her hands. Her nails were smooth with rising moons. She pressed on his cheek and he blushed. He imagined the rough hands of a stranger and felt the weight of a baby in his own arms.

When he asked what happened to the child, they were forced to be direct. Martin stared at the milk until it made him cry. His mother left the table and returned with a bottle of chocolate syrup. She poured some into his glass and swirled it with a tall spoon.

'Our love for you,' she said, 'will always be stronger than any truth.

He was allowed to sleep in their bed for a few days, but then missed his toys and the routine in which he had come to recognize himself fully.

A short time later his sister, Yvette, was born.

When Yvette was six years old and Martin a teenager, they closed the bakery and left Paris for California.

Martin never quite understood why they waited so long to apply for adoption papers. Then, when he was a freshman at a small college in Chicago, smoking in bed with a lover, the curtain was lifted.

It was snowing. They ordered Chinese food. A good film was about to start on television. As Martin reached for the ashtray, the sheet uncovered his body. His legs were so muscular. She laid her cheek against them. He told her about West Hollywood High School, track records still unbroken. She listened, then confessed how she was curious, had been wondering why, unlike other European men, Martin was circumcised.

He stopped attending classes.

He read until his eyes were unable to focus.

He was outside the library when it opened and worked until closing. When the director found out what he was doing, she gave him a space in the staff refrigerator. He requested books with titles no one could pronounce. Every photograph was a mirror.

The semester came to an end, and he went home to Los Angeles.

His parents knew he would find out eventually, but couldn't tell him anything new. His small clothes had been too soiled to keep.

He went to the beach with his sister and watched her swim. He sat on the stairs and listened to his family watch television. He took long drives in the middle of the night.

He worked at the family café. They sold croissants and fruit tarts in boxes tied with blue-and-white twine.

One afternoon, after making deliveries, Martin returned to find the front door of the shop locked with the blinds pulled down. After entering through the back door, he was surprised to find the kitchen in darkness. When he reached the counter, the lights came on suddenly and a roomful of people shouted, 'Surprise!'

Everyone was dressed up, and there were balloons tied to the chairs. People kissed him on the cheek and forehead. Many of the customers he'd known for years were there, and some of the men wore skullcaps. Music came on and people clapped.

Martin was stunned. 'I don't understand,' he said. 'Has something happened?'

'We just thought we'd give you a kind of coming-of-age celebration,' his mother said.

'It's tradition in many cultures,' his father added.

After that, Martin's story was told at every dinner table in Beverly Hills. People came in just to meet him, to tell him *their* stories, to show him photographs, to convince him that he was not alone – that he would never be alone. One day a woman came into the shop and just stood at the counter in front of Martin. Then she started screaming, 'My son! My son! My son!'

Martin's parents took her into the back and gave her hot tea. Then his father drove her home, where her sister was waiting in the driveway.

Sundays were the busiest days.

Martin served customers and decorated birthday cakes with a plump funnel of icing. He felt light-headed at the endless list of names, each one a small voice; each one a thumping heart, but louder, deeper, and more permanent now in its silence.

He had been reborn into the nightmare of truth. The history of others had been his all along. The idea of it was more than he could bear. People hiding in the sewers; women giving birth in the dark, in the damp and filth, then suffocating their babies so as not to give the others away.

Families ripped apart like bits of paper thrown into the wind.

They all blew into his face.

Martin decided not to go back to college, so his father revealed the mysteries of flour, water, heat, and time. He shared recipes from old postcards of tiny writing. Audrey Hepburn sometimes drank coffee in the back with his mother. She laughed and held the mug with both hands. Arthur Miller and his sister, Joan, came in for tea and madeleines. The café was famous for running out of things to sell, and often closed by 3:00 p.m.

Martin was a good son. He worked hard and looked after his parents. For him, there was nothing to forgive. He told his mother this on her deathbed in 2002.

'My love for you,' he said, 'will always be stronger than any truth.'

II.

THEY HAD MOVED to California when Martin was a teenager.

It all started when a global human rights organization sent a telegram to their Paris apartment. His mother was to be recognized publicly as a hero for her actions in 1943 and 1944. Martin and Yvette cheered and drew pictures. They wondered what she could have done that was so brave, but after supper she burned the letter in the sink. Martin's father opened a window and washed away the charred scraps.

A few weeks later, a certificate arrived with her name in gold. There was also an invitation to something official. When she failed to respond, a lawyer showed up in the middle of dinner one night. They asked him to come back another time, but he insisted.

'I tell you I wasn't in the Resistance,' Martin's mother kept saying. 'It must have been another Anne-Lise.'

'That's right,' his father said. 'We weren't even in Paris during the war. The family bakery was closed.'

'But I have proof,' the lawyer insisted, opening his briefcase.

Martin and his sister were sent to their rooms. They tried to listen through the door but were soon distracted.

A few hours later they changed into their bedclothes and crept out to the kitchen. Their mother had been crying. The lawyer was quiet and slumped in his chair. When he saw Martin and his sister in the doorway, he stood up to leave.

He thanked them for the meal, then looked around at the peeling paint, the uneven floors, the boiled white tablecloth, and the less expensive cut of meat they had served him with wine he drank out of courtesy.

'There is also a sizable monetary award,' he told

them at the door, 'to go with the certificate, which I'm afraid will be impossible to refuse.'

They used half the money to emigrate, and the other half to open the Café Parisienne in an area of Los Angeles that seemed friendly and calm in 1955.

The café is still open today and run by Martin's sister, Yvette. The regulars say *bonjour* and *merci*, but that's the limit of their French. The walls are crowded with signed photographs and Christmas cards collected over the years. Tourists take pictures with camera phones. Yvette plays jazz on the radio, and the net curtains his mother hung are still in the window. The bell above the door is from their old shop in Paris, which became a launderettte that goes all night.

Martin sees his sister once a week. Sometimes they walk around the block, or sit down and eat something. He always leaves with a cake, which he lays on the backseat of his station wagon.

His drive home is a long road with many lights. Sometimes people next to him glance over. When he smiles, they mostly look away. But Martin likes to think they carry his smile for a few blocks – that even the smallest gesture is something grand.

For a long time now, he has been aware that anyone in the world could be his mother, or his father, or his brother or sister.

He realized this early on, and realized too that what people think are their lives are merely its conditions. The truth is closer than thought and lies buried in what we already know.

III.

MARTIN'S DUTIES AT the Starlight Retirement Home are numerous, but days grant only a fraction of their possibility. Residents buzz at the slightest provocation: the sink is draining too slow; the lightbulb has gone and I can't see; the window is stuck and I need some air; I can't work the DVD or find the remote; I can't find my glasses either and believe they've been stolen; the flowers my son brought last week need fresh water and the vase is too heavy.

They close their eyes when he brushes their hair. Some want a goodnight kiss or to be held. Martin cares for them without seeming to age. When he changes their sheets in the night, they watch as he wrestles the mattress. He reassures them and stays until they feel tired again.

There is always an assortment of coloured pills beside the bed, and photographs of the long dead in heavy frames. On the desk: newspapers folded carefully, social announcements, bingo schedules, Medicaid forms, invitations to graduation ceremonies, and other records of achievement.

It's all happening again but for someone else.

Today, Martin carries a bucket of plastic letters down the corridor. It's very early – only the whirr of air conditioning through floor vents. The canteen is empty but smells of food and carpet freshener. The carpet is thin so wheelchairs and walkers glide smoothly. There is a place to park them away from the tables. Some of the residents are proud and have not adapted well.

It's January, but California is always sunny. The brown leather sandals that Martin wears make him look gentle. His feet are ash white, and the hairs on each foot come alive in the bathtub. He likes to stare at his body in the water. A long time ago in Paris, it was given away by a faceless man on a crowded street to become an object of desire for his late wife.

Sometimes he closes his eyes and sinks.

In the darkness, behind a veil of thought, there is always someone to meet him.

Long ago, when he was invisible, Martin swam from one person into another. He was alone, but for the echo of that other heart.

The absence later would require a God.

After long days of small problems, Martin lifts his feet from the sandals and soaks them in a basin of warm water with antiseptic that his sister orders from France.

Most nights, he watches television. Then he falls asleep and the television watches him. When there is wind or rain, he turns everything off and opens a window.

He was married for thirty-four years.

They lived in Pasadena. The memories keep him company. He doesn't believe in finding anyone new. He's happy with what he had. Desire is met with the memory of satisfaction.

The white letters in the bucket are made of plastic. Thin roots anchor them to a message board pocked with holes. The letters speak without a speaker. Martin closes the frame and stands back.

There are knives chopping in the kitchen. Laughter. The thread of a radio. With the sign in his arms, he wonders if he should have carried it to the entrance of the dining hall *before* applying the letters. But logic barely applies in this instance: each letter weighs only the same as a matchstick.

A new resident arrived on Friday from England.

Martin remembers seeing him in the hallway because his head is severely disfigured. He arrived in the back of a white Mercedes with only a suitcase. There was a young man with him, a son or grandson whom some of the residents recognized from the movie business.

When he was growing up in Paris, there was an alley behind the bakery and a park opposite. Martin was allowed to go there and run around. Rough boys from the housing estates sometimes threw stones or chased him into the alleyway. Priests from a nearby seminary perched on the benches in twos and threes. They hissed at the bullies and shook their fists. In winter, the priests wore long coats and shared cigarettes.

The homeless slept at one end of the park as a group, then rolled out across the city at first light.

Martin sometimes took them food. His father always scolded him, but never told him to stop doing it.

One of those men had a disfigurement too. He hardly spoke and never came forward, so Martin made sure he brought enough for everyone.

So much has happened since then, yet nothing has changed. Martin sees the same men on benches in Santa Monica, and though their faces are different, they eat their day-old pastries from the Café Parisienne with the same expression.

The sign is finished, but one of the letters is too low and falls out of the word as if trying to flee.

COME WELCOME NEW RESIDENT
MR HUGO
3PM TODAY
STARLIGHT LOUNG E

Martin had planned to watch motor racing in his room. Saturday afternoon is usually his. But twenty minutes won't hurt, and there will probably be sandwiches and cookies. The new resident, Mr Hugo, might even have an interesting story. Maybe he too was once married and is now forced to live alone. Maybe his childhood is a mystery. We all have different lives, Martin believes – but in the end probably feel the same things, and regret the fear we thought might somehow sustain us.

IV.

AFTER OPENING ALL the windows in the canteen, Martin checks the ice machine because it jams. He wants to go back upstairs and make toast with the television on, but all the table vases are empty. Mrs Doyle insists on flowers. This makes more work in the garden, but Martin doesn't mind because it keeps things cheerful and reminds him of his late wife.

There is a pond near the garden. It attracts dragonflies. Sometimes Martin sets down his wheelbarrow and follows them to the edge. Water conjures the surface of an afternoon, but remembers nothing.

He cuts an armful of purple flowers and carries them inside.

Mrs Doyle arrives sometime after lunch. The windows are closed because the air conditioning is on. Martin can hear laughing in the kitchen. Mrs Doyle will be pleased that he went out of his way to cut flowers and that he's wearing a tie. It makes her look professional, she says – as do filled vases, and a functioning ice machine.

Martin can hear Mrs Doyle in the kitchen, but her voice is soon covered by the scream of a metal tank that boils water. Steam and scalding drops. The chatter of cups turned over. She bundles through double doors with a platter of food. Lettuce staggered along the edge. Radishes carved into bloom like Arctic flowers. The sandwiches are cut into triangles. The tablecloth is a stiff, dumb white. Purple flowers in vases of clear water.

Chef appears with a tray of teacups and saucers. His turban is yellow. His wife works in the kitchen too. Once a day they go outside to argue. Mrs Doyle tries to straighten the letter in the message board, then gives up.

Martin imagines what he would be doing otherwise: the ascending pitch as engines tear across the asphalt. Hot tires. A grey track streaked with black lines. As Chef pours tea, somewhere in the world, thousands of people cheer as men steer cars around the racetrack. The sound is deafening, but the drivers hear nothing. They wear white cotton balaclavas under their helmets. The weight of the helmets won't be felt until after the race, when shoulders burn.

In the arms of their wives and lovers, they will recount the drama of a single bend, the spike of concern for a driver whose car is in bits.

As old men, they will dream of this afternoon in their beds – jaws clenched as frail feet press ghost pedals.

Martin chews a sandwich. The cucumber is sliced thin and mixes well with the butter. Bursts of crying from the kitchen, then more laughter. One of the cooks had a baby and brings her in on Saturdays. Mrs Doyle doesn't mind. All her children are grown. Most of the residents are delighted. Many want to hold it, but are not allowed, so they cradle it in their minds instead, and remember the lives they once inhabited.

About three o'clock, the new resident, Mr Hugo, appears. His head is badly deformed. Martin wonders if he fought in World War II. He looks old enough. His mouth is open and breathing is laboured, but he walks without hesitation towards the table of sandwiches. His eyes are milky grey and probably don't see the purple flowers. Then his legs suddenly fold and he drops to the floor.

Martin rushes over. Mrs Doyle is frantic. Chef sprints towards the kitchen shouting his wife's name, but the old man has only a minute or so left.

Martin reaches under his body and cradles him like

a child. He is breathing and conscious, but his eyes are rolling around. There is blood because he bit his tongue.

Martin has seen this before. He reassures the man that help is coming, and the new resident steadies his eyes. Martin's gaze must not falter because there's always fear.

He strokes the old man's hair and holds him tight. When Martin hums a song he remembers from long ago, the old man's eyes sparkle with recognition. His head is deformed because many years ago he was shot in the face.

There are signs for what is coming. Martin leans down and whispers the words his late wife whispered to him during her final moments.

Then, breathing slowly and, almost deliberately, stops. But for a moment the old man doesn't realize he is dead. He can feel Martin's heart and mistakes it for his own.

V.

MARTIN WENT BACK to his seat when the paramedics arrived. Mrs Doyle watched them load the body and chatted with the medical examiner, who wrote things on a clipboard.

'He's gone to a better place,' she said.

'Not everyone believes in God, Mrs Doyle,' the examiner remarked.

'That doesn't matter, Doctor,' she reassured him. '*He'll* catch him in His net.'

The race Martin wanted to see is over. People screaming as drivers pour champagne over each other's heads.

Outside, a few residents are talking on the bench beside the pond. This is something they never get used to.

Martin imagines taking off his clothes and giving his weight to the water. The bottom is soft, and his feet sink in the soggy darkness.

He dips beneath the surface and opens his eyes. It stings but he can see.

He was given to his mother by a man he can't even imagine.

He assumes the best because he knows so little.

The Starlight Retirement Home did not exist back then. Los Angeles was a suburb of voluptuous cars and hamburger stands. It was always hot and there was dust.

At night, puffs of neon lit the streets.

Mr Hugo's body is being taken away.

We cross from memory into imagination with only a vague awareness of change.

The carpet in the canteen where the old man died was once shallow forest. Beyond that – a slow river where lions drank in gulps, water dripping from their mouths.

In the distance, smoke from fires of dried grass.

The people here collected acorns and shellfish. They killed deer and small animals.

Buried under the Starlight pond are the bones of a woman, famous in the tribe for performing ancestral songs. When she sang them by the fire, no one moved.

The person she loved most was her daughter. They liked to arrange feathers. Others would stop what they were doing and watch.

The curb where the ambulance is parked is where the woman's daughter once found a small bird.

She waited all day for its mother, then at dusk, carried the animal back to her home.

Other children ran to see what she had, and there was general excitement.

MR HUGO

MANCHESTER, ENGLAND,

1981

I.

I WOULD LOOK UP from the television and see Danny's face at the window. I motioned with my hand, *Come in, come in.* Door handle turned itself.

He made me watch children's programmes. Then evening came. We shared something hot to eat. Always *Thank you, Mr Hugo.* Polite boy, Danny was.

I met Danny after he moved in next door. I worked nights at the Manchester Royal Infirmary then. Sometimes I would finish all my work before the shift ended. I would sit and read. Drink coffee. Watch night drain.

I lived in a terraced house. Next door was empty six months before Danny and his mother moved in. I remember walking home with bags of shopping, stopping to look through the front window. The sadness of empty rooms.

One day a van pulled up. I watched through the curtains.

A procession of chairs, beds, and boxes. Men in overalls. At lunchtime, the men sat and ate something. Then they drank tea and closed their eyes.

Later in a brown car a woman and boy arrived.

I met the woman on our doorsteps a few days later, bringing in the milk and eggs. She held up a bottle of chocolate milk.

'It's my son Danny's birthday today,' she said. 'We just moved in.'

I nodded.

She was from Nigeria and spoke English gently, words handed, not thrown. She came to England with her parents as a girl in the 1950s.

It's cold here, and dark in winter. Always raining too.

I sat quietly thinking. A boy's birthday next door. The television was on, but I was elsewhere. A balloon was tied to the front door. It bobbed at my window when the wind caught it. Children arrived with their parents about three, then went home a few hours later very tired (some were crying). I watched all through the curtains.

Sometimes I left tomatoes on her doorstep. I grew them myself in the greenhouse. The English like to fry tomatoes for breakfast.

The night I first met Danny, I was woken up by the doorbell. I was frightened because it was late.

Danny was holding his mother's hand and wearing

pyjamas. A blue robe tied at the middle. I had never met the boy before but heard noises through the wall: jumping on the bed, jumping off the bed. Shouting. And when he was sick, coughing all night kept us both up.

'Sorry to disturb you so late, Mr Hugo,' she said, 'but I have a bit of an emergency.' The boy was trying not to stare at my misshapen head. His mother must have warned him. It frightens everyone at first. But over time, you get used to almost anything.

I touched the bristles of my chin.

'I absolutely have to go out, Mr Hugo. It's work, but I can't leave my son home on his own – would you mind?'

I nodded yes.

'Thank you so much; he's a good boy.'

His mother leaned down:

'This is Mr Hugo, Danny, who leaves those delicious tomatoes for us.'

'But I hate tomatoes,' the boy said with sleep in his eyes. There were racing cars on his pyjamas. His small hands didn't know where to go.

The night was cold, and our three bodies moved in the darkness.

'It's really an emergency; just put him on the sofa for a few hours, he won't be any trouble.'

She turned to go.

'Danny-be-good-boy-for-Mummy.'

I led the boy into the sitting room. He looked at his feet. I told him to sit. Then I put the lights on.

'Suppose you want tea?'

He nodded yes.

The kettle rose to a boil. I watched him through the serving hatch.

'What's your name again?'

'Danny.'

'How old are you?'

'Seven.'

'Want sugar?'

Nodded yes.

'How many?'

'Five lumps.'

'That's a lot.'

'I know.'

I sat opposite him in a deep chair. We held mugs and sipped. I considered putting the radio on but didn't.

Then the boy said:

'Excuse me, but what time is it?'

'Late.'

'How late?'

'Very.'

'Then it's early, isn't it? It's so late it's early again,' he said.

I nodded yes.

'What's the emergency for your mother?'

'Mum looks after old people, and sometimes they need her at night – like if they fall down the stairs or die.'

'Who looks after you?'

'Janice. She lives next door on the other side.'

'Where is Janice?'

'Dunno.'

'Where is your father?'

'Dunno. Mum said he works on an oil rig.'

'You met him?'

'Not yet.'

We sat up talking, then fell asleep where we were. His mother came late the next morning. I was turning sausages in the pan. The doorbell rang. She had cans of lager in a white plastic bag and looked tired.

'Here you go,' she said, handing over the bag. 'Just to say thanks.'

The ground was black with rain. Danny's slippers squeaked on the doorstep. The house was quiet again.

I went upstairs.

Sat in my bedroom.

Drew the curtains.

Lay down with my eyes open.

Quite soon, I saw Danny dragged from his bed.

The officers kept order.

Screams outside, then gunfire. Neighbours peek into the street through lace curtains. Danny is separated from his mother. It's not in black and white like films, but in colour like real life.

Different people are pulling his arms. His slipper comes off, then his mother is shot in front of him. Her head opens. Something white. Her hair is clumped. Danny's small fists closing and opening.

It's how we might have met. It's the job I *could* have been given. Something I could have been ordered to do but wasn't. I did other things. I wore the uniform. I marched. Saluted the *Führer.* Loaded my weapon. Fired my weapon. And there was always blood, always somebody's blood.

I vomited on the carpet. A thick paste. I fingered my coarse grey hair and the bare, misshapen area where nothing grows.

I stood in a cold shower. Lost feeling.

Those days, I often punished myself, but nothing changed.

Downstairs, I stared at the almost empty teacups

on the counter. Still warm. I conjured his slippers. His small feet. Racing-car pyjamas. His gentle eyes asking, *Where is your head?* There was something to him, like the boy in Paris who brought cakes to the park for me and the other homeless ones.

Now another child.

No:

Another small God. And Mr Hugo is the child over there, on the sofa, with tea, and someone to sit with in silence, night passing.

I had been woken from my dream by someone else's.

II.

DANNY USUALLY CAME after school. His mother didn't mind because she worked late. I made something for him to eat. Danny's favourite was fish fingers, beans, and American-style french fries. He took the french fries from the freezer, then arranged them on an oven tray. The fish fingers had to be cooked slowly or were cold in the middle. Danny watched television, laughing from time to time. I listened through the serving hatch and felt light, felt unafraid.

Then we ate together. A man and boy eating: I felt echoes from long ago. The knife and fork were too big for Danny. I thought of *the* knife. Remembered *the* knife. My father kept it on the mantelpiece. I should have buried it. Then Danny interrupts. Always more ketchup, Mr Hugo, always more brown sauce. He puts vinegar on his french fries, then on mine. I don't like vinegar, but it's too late and would just hurt his feelings. Danny always saved one fish finger for last. I never knew why.

I cleared up after he left. Sometimes I left the dinner plates until next morning. Beans hardened against the ceramic were almost impossible to remove, but I felt light, felt unafraid.

One afternoon, Danny brought new pencils, and so before children's programmes, we made drawings.

'Your clouds are good. It's like you stole them from the sky.'

Silence.

Strokes on paper like sighing.

'That's impossible,' he said.

'What is?'

'To steal clouds.'

'I know, I just meant it's a nice drawing.'

'I draw a lot in school. I wish we just drawed all day but we don't.'

'What else do you do?'

'Dunno,' he said.

'You don't know?'

'Stuff that's too hard.'

'Like what?'

'Like reading. I'm just not good.'

I thought for a moment. 'Many things are hard, Danny. Life comes at you in pieces sometimes too big to avoid.'

He seemed hurt.

Dinner was boil-in-the-bag fish. Peas. Bread and butter.

I watched him push peas off the plate. He said he didn't like fish when I knew he did. I think I understood then what was going on.

His mother hadn't come by the time *Carry on Laughing* had finished. The ten o'clock news started. We listened to Big Ben and the headlines. Danny said everything in the world was going wrong.

Then his mother called. She said the old person she looked after was still bad.

I asked Danny if we might draw a little more. His eyes were fixed on the television.

'Mum will be here soon,' he said.

'Come, Danny, let's draw, because there's something I can't figure out.'

'What's that?'

'Just lines.'

'Lines?' he asked. 'The ones you draw?'

I nodded yes.

'Lines are easy,' he said. 'Want me to teach you how to do them?'

By midnight, when his mother rang the bell, we had pages and pages of lines in felt-tip pen.

'They're not as straight as I wanted,' Danny said. 'But you get the idea.'

'They're straight enough for what I am doing.'

'What are you doing that needs not-straight lines?'

'A book.'

'What's it called?'

'The book of lines.'

A week later we worked on curved lines. Then after that we played games with sounds, and gave each shape its own voice. We marvelled at how the shapes can tell you that someone is hungry, cold, afraid, bored, or disappointed.

I tried to convey to the boy how people's lives are often altered by curved lines read slowly from paper, sand, or stone.

Danny listened to all.

Weeks passed until, tying lines into shapes with his pencil, Danny recognized them from school and was suddenly reluctant to go on.

I'm not proud to admit that I bribed him with bars of chocolate, but we were so close by then – he knew the voice of each letter, and so it was just a matter of confidence, which would come with practise.

Two months later, a breakthrough over bedtime drinks.

After ten minutes of staring at a container of chocolate powder, the word *instant* burst through Danny's small lips.

He ran around the house screaming.

Not long after that, his mother gave me permission to take him to the library, where Danny taught Mr Hugo about dinosaurs, comets, gold miners, and steam.

When Danny turned twelve, his mother fell in love with a Scottish man, and they moved to Glasgow. He was doing well in school by then, and had a special friend called Helen. She had red hair and a deep voice. Her father worked in a bank. A very important man, Danny said. They came around after school. A polite boy, Danny was – always made sure she had enough to drink, enough to eat, and somewhere to rest her feet when they watched television. He must have explained early on that Mr Hugo's head might shock, because when we met, Helen's first words were: 'Isn't it nice how people are all different?'

She didn't ask what happened, and I'm glad she didn't because I can't remember everything. I know I woke up in a French hospital in a body I didn't recognize. I know some of the things I had done because there were faces that haunted me. And I know that the missing part of my skull was in Paris, splintered into pieces too small to find.

After Danny and his mother moved away, life was quiet again.

Television, weather, tomatoes, nightmares . . . watching all through the curtains.

Then. One morning, a month into the silence, I woke in the early hours. Winter, but I went outside and stood on the back patio.

The air was frigid. I moved my arms in the silvery outline of dawn.

Could smell rain coming.

A stick of Danny's chalk glowed from a crack in between the paving.

I got down on my hands and knees and drew straight lines on the stones with the chalk. Then I drew curved lines and made letters. Then I bunched letters into words and made sentences. Soon the patio was covered:

> . . . Swing of Danny's legs from park benches. Frying chips and putting ketchup on them. Running up and down the stairs. Mother's shoes on doorstep moment before bell. Socks coming off. Spoon stirring tea. Drying forks and putting them in the drawer. An anchor of hair on his forehead. Hot chocolate. Falling asleep in chairs. Danny's face at the window. The door handle turning itself. Squeaking slippers on the step. Kettle rising gently to a boil.

Rain fell but I kept going.

Soon the drops were falling faster than my hand could write, but I went on, I continued until there was nothing to see, nothing to read, nothing but the single moment of pressure with nothing before and nothing after.

This was Danny's gift.

SÉBASTIEN

SAINT-PIERRE, FRANCE,

1968

I.

SÉBASTIEN LOOKS OUT the classroom window, but doesn't see passing cars, or brown leaves like claws on the pavement attached to nothing. He can reach for things without touching them. Thinking and desire are one.

After school, he will take Hayley to see the iron skeleton he found in the woods. He wants to find a corner of the playground and hug her all lunchtime – hug her so tightly that she becomes a part of him. Instead, later on, she will trail him through the woods to the skeleton behind the farm. There she will love him the way he has seen in films, especially the ones he watches with Grandma on Saturday afternoons, when the room flickers and the music is heavy. The actors' faces are soft and grey. It begins with a single dance. And then a telephone call.

Unwashed sheets hang in the sky. They smell of salt from the sea. It's been raining since early morning, but will turn to snow when the bell rings.

Sébastien awoke to rain on the window like a thousand eyes. The wind was gusting. Birds blown off course. Teddies blown out of bed. They all have names and behave differently. He likes to hold one at night. It gets him through.

The lights in the classroom are always bright and warm. The class mice, Tik and Tok, are sleeping. Their fur is tight. Sébastien's hair sticks up in the morning. Only water keeps it down.

He likes to draw for ten minutes before school. Sometimes when he sharpens his colouring pencils, the lead breaks off and he's back where he started. His mother shouts at him to get dressed, but he's looking at the hollow socket. He can feel what is not there.

His drawing is unfinished.

The outline of another world.

He feels this one by imagining others.

Play is where he recognizes himself.

Closing his bedroom door on one life because there are so many.

His mother shouts at him to get dressed. He indignantly stands, driven by the engine of his heart.

The tyranny of school.

The shuffle of toast and the scrape of butter.

The kettle driving ghosts into the world.

Resting his feet on the dog's back under the table. The dog won't move as long as crusts or bits of sausage appear from time to time.

It's so early, but his father is already out on the tractor.

The school corridor smells of milk and coats. The sound of boots being taken off. Sometimes socks come off, too. Like children, they don't want to leave home.

The fear of being lost.

The fear that never goes away and cannot be dispelled.

Then the bell and a list of names called out. Sébastien knows it by heart and whispers it in bed, like a prayer of parentheses. Desks opening and closing like mouths. Scribbled messages on the back of the seat in front of him. He feels the teacher's unhappiness. It's in how she stands, how she moves, her hair, her clothes.

The lesson will end one day. A ringing bell means glory, freedom, something to run for. He can go home and sit at the table with nothing to do. He can venture into woods and look for animals. He can visit the skeleton, and drum on its hard skin.

He can set up his LEGO train and lay people underneath to fix the engine. He can close his curtains and put his torch in a sock. Moonlight spills across the train yard. Little plastic men and women go home to hot plastic dinners. They walk quickly to keep warm.

They are like us, but smaller. They are like us

with things in their pockets, and good moods and bad moods, and spontaneous moments of love and cruelty. They yawn. They too lie awake, unable to sleep, going over arguments or unravelled by desire. They give birth to plastic babies, whose fathers work in the train yard. Even at night, the train must be repaired.

Nobody knows why it broke down in the North Pole at midnight. Perhaps a miracle will occur before supper, and Hayley's family will not freeze in the Arctic tundra of white bedsheet and aluminium-foil lake.

Sébastien looks out the classroom window. The teacher is talking but says nothing. Her heart is asleep. His heart is asleep. The children's hearts are asleep and will remember nothing.

He imagines himself in the black metal shell of his skeleton house – a home they will soon share. He is sitting in the heavy seat that long-ago fathers sat in – when the great skeleton flew. Sébastien knows from old films. He's seen them in the air. When the world was grey. The men who flew his skeleton wore masks. You could hear them breathing.

It was not Sébastien's France then, not a country of brioche and endless school trips to the windy beach with the caravan in summer – but a country of mud, and women in aprons watching the giant skeletons pass above, spitting bullets into the guts of other skeletons.

Children then must have stood around in puddles wondering when their parents would come home, looking up at the sky for metal drops, or down at themselves in the grey water. They were barefoot and thin. Sébastien has seen it on television. And his grandmother has told him.

Sébastien feels what he has never experienced: houses on fire, dogs barking at people trying to hide. He has seen pictures in books too. He knows something happened long ago – something bad. He can see it in the eyes of the children who live in the pages.

He wants to take Hayley into the metal belly of his secret house. It lies sleeping in the woods behind his family farm. It yawns when you knock. Although his mother once told him not to go too deep into the endless woodland at the far end of the cow pasture, he genuinely forgot. By then it was too late. As recompense, he does his chores. He helps Papa with the cows on Sunday and forces down Brussels sprouts. He gets dressed after being asked three times, and doesn't leave LEGO pieces everywhere.

It gets dark quickly in the weeks leading up to Christmas. People go to bed early. Winter is for dreaming.

Moonlight sharpens the garden outside Sébastien's window. He opens his window a crack. The cold fills his bedclothes like a flapping tongue. He listens for animals and sometimes hears them. Sparkling lines of tinsel tie the house together. Cards hang on strings above the fireplace.

Hayley has agreed to play.

She said yesterday she would come over. That's when he thought:

SHOW HER THE SKELETON

Take her into the woods, why not?

She will glow as she walks around. His pleasure has doubled already. She will not want to go home. She will have questions, he knows that. There are things he wants to know too. Why did it crash? Where was it from? If there are real skeletons in there, he hasn't found them. Did the skeletons not in there have children? Are they skeletons now because of time? Maybe the skeletons are in the trees. He's heard of that. It was in the news once.

He knows you have to be older to marry. It's so sad because he's ready now. And then you find a house and then babies are given to you carefully in towels at the hospital. Their tiny lips say *who*.

But at least there are damp flat cushions in the back where it's very dark. Light only reaches its fingers in so far. The windshield in the front is split into pieces like a spider's eyes. Some of them are broken. Some are too dirty to see out of.

When it rains, the skeleton dreams of gunfire. Sometimes Sébastien sits in the seat where the gun handle is and pretends to shoot cows grazing silently in the dusk, beyond the trees. He imagines steaming parcels of roast beef in every place where a cow was. Then he fires upon the potatoes. Brussels sprouts cut to shreds.

When he first discovered it, he was too afraid to go inside. He kept patting the black skin and listening to the echo. He looked around for the second wing but couldn't find it. Then he peed on a wheel with a flat tire that's close to a pile of twisted black metal and decided to go in where it's split.

Sébastien marvels at how it cut through thick trees, then plowed the earth with its glass nose.

His father said the forest beyond the pasture is too expensive to clear. His family bought the farm when Sébastien was one. His father was an attorney in Paris. He met Sébastien's mother on a train to Amsterdam. There were no other seats. They were forced together and found they preferred it. His mother came from Normandy and dreamed of staying in the country.

After they were married, they looked for places where they could make a living.

The teacher sometimes stops talking, and when Sébastien looks over, she is already looking at him, which means: Why are you looking through the window and not at me? But Sébastien is not looking through the window, but through the scrapbook of things that have pierced his heart.

Lives are staged from within.

Sébastien wants to make a little home for Hayley in the skeleton. They can sit in the old seat and press buttons. There is dust and mud and oil on everything, the smell of something heavy, dripping, and tick, tick, tick. (Also groaning.)

There are dials and switches and things to hold and pull. All the bits must remember what happened. They keep each other company but say nothing.

Sébastien found something else under the seat, a leather case with brown cards and the photograph of a woman.

The secret fills his mouth like cotton wool, but if he tells, it might be taken away. He might be famous (local newspaper or television) for finding it, true – but if fame takes away the thing it celebrates, then Sébastien would prefer the inspired silence. We're all famous in our own hearts anyway.

Yes, it is snowing.

Three-year-olds are screaming.

Others rush past to be in it. Sébastien is leaning against the wall of the canteen hut. Some of the children are laughing and kicking snow. It's annoying how they copy one another.

Parents are chatting and smoking.

Cars hum along the road by the gates. The glow of brake lights.

Hayley.

Her eyes are deep and dark. Her hair is combed neatly to one side. She doesn't say anything, but smiles. A few of her teeth are missing. Her shoes are never scuffed like his. Her backpack has a cat on it. Hayley loves cats. She has a kitten and Sébastien has played with it once in real life, but in his imagination they are brothers and the cat talks and tells him about life in Hayley's house.

'I can't play today,' she says.

'You have to.'

'*Maman* is picking me up.'

'Why is she?'

'I'm going to the dentist.'

'Why?'

'I don't know.'

'Can't you go tomorrow?'

Hayley shrugs. 'I'll ask.'

'I want to show you something you won't believe.'

'Show me tomorrow.'

'It has to be today. It has to be now.'

'Why?'

'Because.'

Hayley's mother appears in the distance, waving.

'You can bring your cat if you like.'

'Okay. Where is it?'

'You'll see.'

'Can we go tomorrow?'

'What about today?'

'I already told you.'

Hayley's mother is almost upon them.

'Take something, then,' Sébastien says, fumbling in his pocket. He holds up a small, wrinkled black-and-white photograph of a woman. Hayley grabs it from him. *Finally, Sébastien and I are married.*

They both drop into the photograph, past white threads where the image has creased. The young woman in the picture doesn't notice. In the background a hot-dog stand and a Ferris wheel.

The woman tilts back her head.

Her smile is changing into a laugh.

Sébastien found the photograph under a seat in the glass nose of the skeleton.

'Is it your grandmother?'

'No,' Sébastien says, 'it's you grown up.'

Hayley stares at the photograph. She touches the woman with the tips of her fingers.

'I like my hair,' she says.

'Yeah, me too, it's just like my grandmother's.'

Sébastien turns over the picture. 'It even almost says your name.'

They stare at the chain of letters until her mother comes.

'Goodbye, Harriet,' Sébastien whispers. 'See you tomorrow.'

JOHN

CONEY ISLAND, NEW YORK,

1942

I.

THE FERRIS WHEEL turned slower than normal so girls could kiss their soldiers goodbye.

'Stand still, Harriet, or it's not gonna work.'

John's father had given him a camera.

'It's too windy,' she cried.

John put the camera down and went over to her.

'I really want a picture of you on the boardwalk,' he said.

She pressed her lips against his and pulled his hair.

'Don't go,' she said.

'Don't go?'

'I don't want you to.'

'If I don't go, I can't come back.'

'Don't go,' she said.

They sat on a low wall and looked at the beach. People were lying on towels. It was a hot day. There were bodies in the water. Children eating quietly under canvas umbrellas.

Something was happening, and nobody knew where it would end. The children who played on John's street wanted to know when their fathers would come home, why their neighbours banged on their doors late at night – why people sat crying in the kitchen with the radio on.

When it got late, they held hands and walked towards the subway.

'Can you still take the photo?' Harriet asked.

She straightened her blouse and adjusted her hair. The thought of his not coming back brought them closer.

John steadied his hands and looked through a small hole at the woman in front of him. He had never loved anyone so much. But it was something he could never admit to her.

It was a truth anchored in his heart so that her pain might be less, so that she might find another, get married again, have children, watch them grow, make their lunches, see them off, visit them in college, get old herself, plan retirement, give away all her jewellery to grandchildren, regret nothing – even forget, *even forget* the boy she was first married to, who took her picture at Coney Island, then was blown to bits in his B-24 by antiaircraft guns over the French coast, escape impossible.

The book of their love would be a chapter in her life.

A digression that ends in a rain of metal over wet fields.

Then a moment before the snap of the shutter – a gust of wind lifted John's hat. Harriet screamed and couldn't stop laughing. Behind her, people on the Ferris wheel and the roller coasters were screaming too. You could hear them up and down the seafront, lost forever in that last great afternoon of their lives.

AMELIA

AMAGANSETT, NEW YORK, 2005

I.

WHEN I WAS ELEVEN, we learned that my condition is permanent. Doctors at a hospital on Park Avenue showed my parents thin squares of plastic that proved it. We were all disappointed. And even though my body was no different, it felt different, as though part of me had died; a part of me strangled by a sentence of bad news.

Then we left the hospital and went to Sant Ambroeus on Madison Avenue. The waiter brought gelato. But I couldn't eat. It would take time for hope to melt.

Finally, my father said we were happy before, and that nothing had actually changed. I could tell he didn't believe it and I wanted to scream.

I was wearing a velvet blazer. One of the doctors had said I looked elegant. I told him I was named after Amelia Earhart. When he didn't answer, I knew it was bad news.

I could tell everyone in Sant Ambroeus was looking at me. I needed the bathroom, and my legs were cold. It was raining. People came in shaking their umbrellas.

We live in the Hamptons all year round, and our house is by the sea.

It often rains suddenly, and my mother runs upstairs to open the window in my room. She sits with me on the bed. It's something we've always done. Sometimes her hands smell like dinner. Sometimes I inhale the scent of her make-up as though trying to lift the veil of who my mother is.

Rain says everything we cannot say to one another. It is an ancient sound that willed all life into being, but fell so long upon nothing.

The silence after is always louder. Birds whistle from low branches, tying their wishes in knots. I imagine their hearts and feel one in my hand like a hot seed.

Even though I'm almost twenty-seven, my mother still puts flowers in my room. She arranges them in a heavy vase that sits on my dresser, next to the plastic model of a B-24 bomber that my grandfather John flew in World War II.

The scent of the flowers lingers for a few days as though waiting for an answer.

Tonight I have a date, which is big news in our house. He's picking me up at six o'clock, but I feel like I'm already with him, sitting quietly in his warm truck.

The radio is on but low.

We're somewhere in Sagaponack, or maybe he's driven to Southampton. It's too cold for the beach, so we sit in the parking lot and talk.

He wants to know what it's like being blind.

I confess the smooth coolness of a window – but the idea of glass is something beautiful and unknown.

I ask him to tell me about stars, but what I really want is to be kissed.

Winter evenings out here are quiet.

The air smells of wood smoke and seawater. The Golden Pear Café fills up early with retired bankers and once-famous artists who sit alone by the window, turning the pages of morning.

Most people remember the Hamptons as an unbroken summer. A place of sandwiches and laughter, hot weather, things lost on the beach.

In summer, I sleep with my windows open. Night holds my body in its mouth.

In this second darkness, my desire flings itself upon a world of closed eyes.

Then dreams break against the rocks of morning.

Summer out here is busy with people doing nothing. And the beaches are crowded – except very early, when it's mostly dogs and people who are alone.

I've been going to East Hampton Beach Club

since I was a girl. I know my way around without needing anyone to guide me. It's also where I learned to swim.

Sometimes old people sit on the benches in front of the restaurant facing the sea. They shuffle in their seats as I pass.

My eccentric grandfather John is ninety-something. He was born on Long Island but lives in a mansion in England. My grandmother Harriet died a few years ago. He designed their gravestone with a poem:

Here lie:

Harriet and John Bray

H.B. Born 1920, Connecticut, U.S.A.
Died 2003, East Sussex
J.B. Born 1923, Long Island, U.S.A.
Died 20 – , East Sussex

When days are darkest, the earth enshrines
the seed of summer's birth.
The Spirit of man is a light that shines
deep in the darkness of earth.

Grandpa John is very old now. He says his only wish is to see me happy. After the war he became a millionaire. He also met Charlie Chaplin.

Between May and September, the supermarket in East Hampton smells like sunscreen, and it's hard to find a parking spot. Someone in Bridgehampton once offered my father a hundred dollars for his space as he was filling the meter. My father said he'd give it to him for a kiss. My mother said he should have taken the hundred dollars.

People stay up late too, and from my bed on a Saturday night, I hear the steady rush of cars between East Hampton and Montauk.

Where are people going?

I wonder what they hope will happen and what they are afraid of?

For me it's the same thing and has to do with being loved.

It's very cold here now.

February is quiet except for the wind, which rushes through hollows in the roof. Everything has a voice. Our house was once a flock of trees in the wilderness.

On Saturday I sleep later than my parents.

Sometimes I wake up and lie still enough to hear

a petal drop from the vase of flowers. Sometimes I lie awake and wish there was someone to hear my falling. In the safety of my bed, on a tightrope between waking and dreaming, my fantasies feel so real – only steps away – around a corner that never ends.

My father opens the curtains slowly to unveil the day. Every day is a masterpiece, even if it crushes you. Light spills across my face. I blink but see nothing.

We had more snow overnight. This morning I went with my father to Riverhead for salt and a new shovel. He likes it when I ride with him. We wear hats and gloves. Saturday has always felt hopeful. He treats me like a girl sometimes. I used to hate it when I was in high school, but now I don't mind. He didn't mention my date tonight, but I could tell he was thinking about it. He asked if I needed anything from the outlets.

I have a job in Manhattan and get home at midnight on Fridays when the museum where I work is open late. In summer, the bus is packed, but I've been riding the Jitney for so long I always get a seat. The drivers know me. My mother bakes cookies for them. I've always wondered if they eat them while they're driving. Sometimes when I get off, I'm tempted to sweep the driver's seat with my hand for crumbs.

When we got home from Riverhead, my father poured salt on the steps. I listened as pellets hit the ice. I imagined a head opening and thoughts falling out. Then my father stopped pouring and told me not to use my separate entrance until he's replaced a few of the steps. The truth is that I hardly use it anyway.

When the bag of salt was empty, we went inside. I made two cups of instant coffee. Then we sat at the kitchen table without taking our coats off.

When my mother came downstairs, my father gave her his coffee and went to make another cup. It's one of their customs. Another one is cocktails on Saturday night. Another is staying up late in summer.

My mother was quiet and asked if there was traffic. She said the heat upstairs was on and off.

My mother wanted to know if there's anything I need washed for tonight. I'll be glad when this date is over so things can go back to normal. My father is worried about the roads. He said we can borrow the Range Rover if the weather gets worse.

When the phone rings, we all jump. It's Dave. My father called him earlier to see if he would come over and chop wood, which means talking for hours and my father smoking Dave's cigarettes.

Dave is from Scotland. He worked for many years as a chef on cruise ships. My mother hired him as her part-time driver, but the only person he drives is me. He and my father really get along. They are the same age, but Dave seems much younger. Sometimes Dave comes over and watches television if my parents are away. He has small hands and smells of onions. He is divorced but has an Irish girlfriend called Janet. She lives in Montauk and has a catering company.

Yesterday on the bus, someone was wearing perfume. Sometimes I can smell the person who occupied the seat before me. Whether you know it or not, we leave parts of ourselves wherever we go. I wonder if I should wear perfume tonight for my date. I usually wear it in summer with a lovely dress. I splurge on one dress a year and then wear it to the Parrish Art Museum's summer ball. My mother takes me to Saks. People stop and listen as she describes what's hanging. Eventually, I touch a fabric and think, *That's me, that's Amelia.*

I ride the Jitney into Manhattan five days a week for my job at the Museum of Modern Art. I set up programmes for the blind. But sometimes I just sit at a desk and answer the phone.

Each summer we get new interns. They go out for ice cream on Friday afternoons and come back late. They talk freely about their lives. I like my job. I help create art that people can touch. The blind patrons come once a month. Some have dogs. Those who are partially sighted have a stick with a heavy ball on the end. Sometimes they burst out laughing when things are placed in their hands. When you can't see, the coolness of metal is exhilarating – the weight of something a sudden intimacy.

Guide dogs are given water. It drips from their mouths back into the bowl. Hot tea is served in paper cups. The blind stare straight ahead and talk very carefully, as if their words are part of the exhibit, as if feelings can be dropped and broken.

The poet Emily Dickinson said that nature is a haunted house, while art is a house that tries to be haunted. She was born and died in the same room.

For young members of the museum, there is sometimes a party or an opening. People wear shoes that echo through the galleries. A banquet table is set up. The coat-check line is long enough to fall in love with the person behind you. My mother said it's important I go to these events. Dad sometimes drives into the city to pick me up. Many people leave together. They go on to other things. Their lives cross like strings. My parents want me to meet someone.

I was asked to dance at the last museum party. He was from Dublin and smelled like cigarettes. After our dance, a slow song came on. I waited for him to lead me off, but we kept dancing.

I was quiet in the car on the way home. Dad asked if I was okay. I remember opening the window and letting the world pour in.

Dave once asked me what blind people dream about. Mostly in sound and feeling, I replied. At night I fall in love with a voice, and then wake to a feeling of physical loss. Sometimes I close my eyes to a chorus of 'Happy Birthday!' The smell of cake and the sound of feet under the table. I awake in a body that's too big. I also dream in motion and sensation. My father's boat and the snore of the mast; the rough fabric of the safety harness and the rip of Velcro. The sun on my legs. An endless stretch of water impossible to imagine.

I dream when I'm afraid of something I won't admit.

A recurring nightmare I've had for years is a dream of silence. In the dream I am alone – but then I hear people moving quietly past. No matter how loud I scream or how frantically I reach out with my hands – I am incapable of a connection.

It's my birthday in a few weeks. Most people think I'm younger than I am.

About six years ago, the summer after I turned twenty-one, my father built a separate entrance that leads to my bedroom. My mother thought it was madness. Months of hammering and sawing. The only silence when my father drove to the hardware store in Sag Harbor for something vital. When it was finished, we stood outside. It was very hot, and my father was drinking beer. Then we climbed the steps and went through a door that led to where my closet had been. It was like Narnia, but the opposite way.

He said it was so my guests wouldn't feel obliged to talk to Mom and Dad, but I use it mostly for sitting on when my parents have parties that go on too late. I've never ventured beyond the third step alone in either direction.

I was in love once.

His name was Philip. We met in Montauk on a bench by the dock. I had been invited to a birthday brunch for someone I hardly knew from high school.

My mother said I might as well go. It turned out to be only a few people and ended early. The real party was on the beach the night before, and people were still passed out.

Dave was supposed to pick me up but got stuck in the usual summer traffic. Then someone sat down on the bench next to me. I could feel him looking but said nothing.

A lady on the Jitney once said that I was beautiful. It was a kind thing to say because I will never see my own face. And although this is hard to admit – as I get older I find myself wanting to be touched. Last summer at a party on Shelter Island, I had too much wine and told my mother that I want to give and receive more hugs. She said, 'Oh, Amelia.'

On the way home she didn't speak. I sat on the steps of my private entrance and cried but felt fine in the morning. Dad must have heard something because he drove all the way to Southampton to pick up fresh croissants for breakfast.

When I was young, about fifteen maybe, I dreamed that a boy would wash up on the beach in front of our house. I would sit for a long time listening to the sea.

When I was offered a job at the Museum of Modern Art, my parents worried about my travelling so far into the city each day. There were so many complications because I'm blind. At first, a taxi service had to meet me where the bus stops on Lexington Avenue, but then after six months, MoMA's head of special collections found out what I was doing and told me to use the interns.

The taxi was paid for by Grandpa John. He also sends money to pay Dave – who drives me into the city when I miss the bus (which is about once a week).

For a long time nobody knew where Grandpa John was.

His B-24 Liberator disappeared in the skies above France. It was 1944.

My grandmother Harriet got a telegram and then drove to the diner that his parents owned. They all sipped gin at a table in the back.

After months without any news, men began asking my grandmother out.

They pulled up outside her house in shiny cars.

They wore sleeveless jumpers and kept their hair short.

Harriet went dancing but was always glad to

come home and go to bed with one of John's handkerchiefs.

She read his letters over and over.

She looked at his drawings of plants, and looked up their Latin names.

The fighting intensified after landings on the Normandy beaches.

At night, the skies over Europe blazed with fire and metal. People sat up in bed as curtains flashed.

The Allies were advancing. There were heavy casualties. Every day, someone on Harriet's block lost a son, or a husband, or a brother.

She remembers kissing John outside Lord & Taylor; the way he held her when they danced at Cousin Mabel's wedding – it was like being held for the first time. Driving to Montauk on Sunrise Highway. The rocks beneath their feet and the sweeping tide. The promise of so much ahead. She knew in her heart that being together would always be enough.

She planned to go to Europe when the war was over and search for his remains. She was confident she could find them.

Then one morning someone came to the door with a telegram.

It was stamped Harrington, England.

She opened it, then ran out of the house in her slippers. She was in such a state, it was hard to drive. People thought she was drunk and shook their heads.

When she got to John's parents' diner, she didn't even turn the engine off or close the door.

When she read the letter aloud to a packed restaurant, John's father collapsed.

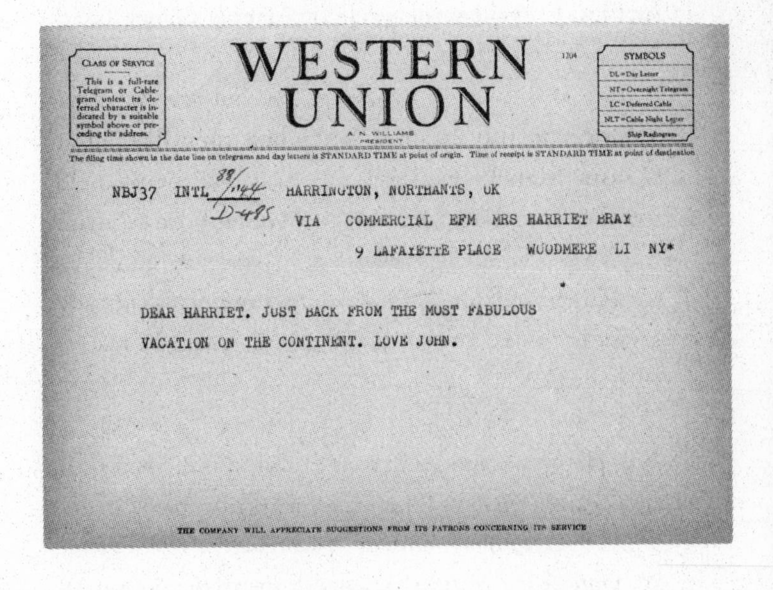

CLASS OF SERVICE

This is a full-rate Telegram or Cablegram unless its deferred character is indicated by a suitable symbol above or preceding the address.

WESTERN UNION

A. N. WILLIAMS
PRESIDENT

SYMBOLS
DL = Day Letter
NT = Overnight Telegram
LC = Deferred Cable
NLT = Cable Night Letter
Ship Radiogram

The filing time shown in the date line on telegrams and day letters is STANDARD TIME at point of origin. Time of receipt is STANDARD TIME at point of destination

NBJ37 INTL 38/1144 HARRINGTON, NORTHANTS, UK
D-485 VIA COMMERCIAL EFM MRS HARRIET BRAY
9 LAFAYETTE PLACE WOODMERE LI NY*

DEAR HARRIET. JUST BACK FROM THE MOST FABULOUS
VACATION ON THE CONTINENT. LOVE JOHN.

THE COMPANY WILL APPRECIATE SUGGESTIONS FROM ITS PATRONS CONCERNING ITS SERVICE

He was home before the war ended, but couldn't stand without help.

Two years later, after fully recovering, John was offered an engineering job in England by one of his RAF friends.

Harriet had never left the East Coast of America, but the English welcomed them with open arms. After a few months, John wrote home and asked his parents to wire his life savings so he could invest in a material to make airplanes lighter and stronger.

My grandpa John would have been one of the richest men in Britain today, Mom says, but he gave most of his fortune away – keeping only what they needed to be comfortable.

In some ways, I think Grandpa John has always felt responsible for my blindness, as if it were something he once wished for himself. He was in the hospital for a long time during the war, and nobody really knows what he saw, or what happened to him after being shot down – not even my grandmother.

His explanation never went beyond the letter.

The first time I remember visiting them in London, my mother had booked a table for a special lunch with just Grandpa and me, and then arranged an afternoon at the Imperial War Museum to see the tanks and the planes.

We were staying at Claridge's Hotel – Grandpa John's treat. I remember waiting on the bed in fancy clothes. My mother was drying her hair. She said it wasn't like him to be late. Eventually, the telephone rang. It was my grandmother. Grandpa John had locked himself in the bedroom and wouldn't come out.

We made up for it in the years ahead, though. Long walks on the beach, bedtime stories that were so long I fell asleep in the middle, cooking brisket from a family recipe.

He also taught me how to dance. It was something he did with my grandmother, even when there was no music. During the war, American servicemen often took local English girls to dances. A few fell in love, but most did it to pass the time. Grandpa John stayed in his bunk and wrote letters to Harriet. He even kept paper and a pencil under his seat in the aircraft for the long flights back to base.

I was named after a pioneer of flight. The last time I told that story was on a bench in Montauk. It was summer and very hot. We were sitting on Gosman's Dock. It was busy with summer people. I had been to a birthday brunch. Children were crying, and laughter spilled from the bars.

Philip was shy at first. I think I asked him to look out for a blue SUV. I told him my father's friend was picking me up.

The summer traffic must have been especially heavy, because we talked for a long time. Sometimes I wonder if Dave wasn't just sitting in the car watching us.

Philip told me what it was like being a fisherman. He said most of what he catches on the boat is for restaurants in Manhattan. He told me it's a hard life, but that it's his life. I asked him if he felt sorry for the fish, and he laughed but gave me a serious answer.

He seemed intelligent. I wondered if he would lie on the beach with me and read poems aloud. I tried to recite a poem from memory about a fish by Elizabeth Bishop, but I only got halfway through.

He asked me if I had ever seen a fish being caught and then quickly apologized. I didn't mind, and explained how I see things clearly in my own way. I see my parents, my garden, my bedroom, my things on the wall, even Dad's boat, even the sea, even a fish being caught.

He asked me more about being blind, but I couldn't think of anything to say. Then a couple wanted us to take their picture.

I was wearing a summer dress from Nanette Lepore

and a pair of sandals. When the couple left, Philip said I had beautiful shoulders. I waited for him to touch them, my heart like a pendulum, swinging between hope and fear.

When Dave arrived, Philip was shy again. We all stood there.

Then Dave and I went to speak at the same time, but I struggled through the embarrassment and told Philip my phone number. Dave offered to write it down, but nobody had a pen.

On the journey back to Amagansett, I couldn't hide from myself. It's as though certain parts inside me broke, but instead of being damaged, I was free. Dave had all the windows open. I could hear his watchband on the door as he tapped to the music. I told him he could smoke if he wanted.

But Philip never called, and the next few months were very hard. It wasn't that I didn't have someone I really liked – but the realization that I had never had anyone.

I was afraid of the sea when I was a girl. Someone said it went on forever and that frightened me. I wondered why my parents had chosen to live at the beginning and the end of the world.

In summer, I go sailing on my father's small yacht. Sometimes I steer while my father looks up from *The New York Times* calling out, 'Leftabit! Rightabit! Leftabit! Now go around the iceberg if you can, Amelia.'

Being blind is not like you would imagine. It's not like closing your eyes and trying to see. I don't feel as though I'm lacking. I see people by what they say to others, by how they move and how they breathe.

We have an apartment on the Upper East Side that we seldom use. It's really Grandpa John's for when he visits. It's close to a café on Madison Avenue called Sant Ambroeus – the place we went after learning that my blindness is permanent.

Grandpa John grew up at a diner on Long Island, but finds it hard to leave England now that he's old.

My mother was raised in England and has an accent. When she was very young, Grandpa John used to wake up screaming. Eventually, Harriet made him go to the village hall once a week for tea with other veterans of World War II. It was a ritual he would keep until he was the only one left. Mom said that whatever they talked about there changed him, and he was suddenly around more, and would dig for potatoes with her in the garden with his suit on, and lie in the mud and make pig noises.

My grandparents really loved each other. I often wonder why they had only one child.

My first time was on the beach at my parents' anniversary party after it got late and people chatted on the terrace in small groups. I was twenty. His name was Julio. He came out with his mother from the city just for the party. I knew him from when we were kids, and his family rented a house all year round a few doors down. Amagansett was so remote then. Our road had only three houses on it.

Back then Julio's mother used to come over and sit on the deck with my mother and drink wine. Julio and I would play for hours. My parents have always liked to drink and talk.

When I was a teenager, they sat me on the couch between them and dropped their wedding album into my lap. They were married in January sometime in the eighties. They had a honeymoon in Tokyo, but spent most of their time in Kyoto – which my father said also told the story of ancient China. They turned the pages slowly. I could hear their fingers on the plastic.

'There's your father eating the first slice of wedding cake.'

'She actually fed it to me,' Dad said. 'Which embarrassed me then, but later I was glad she did it.'

'Why?' my mother wanted to know.

'Because I realized they are my hands now.'

'Your hands!' My mother laughed. 'You're mad.'

I think people would be happier if they admitted things more often. In a sense we are all prisoners of some memory, or fear, or disappointment – we are all defined by something we can't change.

Losing my virginity to Julio after my parents' anniversary party was amazing. He had a girlfriend – but sometimes you have to break rules because nothing is perfect.

Years and years before, when Julio lived close by, he taught me how to ride a skateboard. He held my hand as it rolled along. Then, laughing but determined, I walked it to the top of the hill. Julio was frantic, but I wasn't afraid because I knew the road and would have heard a car. I remember the wheels spitting out small stones. How could I have known the neighbour's boyfriend was out from the city for Passover and parked on the road?

I spent the night in Southampton hospital.

The doctor said I was very lucky. My father said to him, 'You guys always say that,' and the doctor chuckled. Then my mother asked if it was the same emergency room where they brought Marilyn Monroe.

Julio came a bit later with his mother and some flowers. They were like summer in his arms.

I told him he shouldn't have brought flowers – that I wasn't dead yet. But he didn't laugh. Everyone told him to cheer up.

After they'd gone and we were alone, Julio cried and cried. He said his parents were getting a divorce. Three months later they moved out, and Julio went to live in Park Slope. We saw each other from time to time and at my parents' anniversary party, but our friendship was based on the past.

The reason I have a date tonight is because of something that happened on the Jitney last week.

The bus was busy that day. We crawl when there's traffic. I know where we are by the length of the turns and the bumps of railroad tracks.

When sunlight pours into the bus, I put on sunglasses and get sleepy. I feel my eyes closing. Falling asleep is like walking out on a frozen lake. The ice gets thinner and thinner until suddenly you fall through.

When someone sat down next to me, I woke up.

'Hello,' said a voice.

It was a young woman. By the time we were on

the Long Island Expressway, she had explained how she's going to the airport to meet her father for the very first time.

I smiled and said smartly that I'd never seen my father, either.

She touched my hand without realizing I'm blind.

'It doesn't matter,' she whispered. 'He feels you.'

And I suddenly thought of Philip out on the sea.

So long I imagined him, so many days last summer I conjured him on my father's boat with us.

I could feel him cutting through the swell, a bulk of fish in the hull.

Forklifts humming back at the dock.

From my office that morning I called Dave. At first he didn't remember who I was talking about. Then I reminded him about picking me up at Gosman's in Montauk. He asked if I knew Philip's last name.

On the Jitney home that night, Dave called to say he hadn't found anything out – but that Janet was going to ask around. I thanked him but felt defeated. Before hanging up, Dave said that if Janet couldn't find Philip, he'd break up with her.

The next day at work I was summoned from a meeting to take a phone call.

It was an effort for him to talk because there was so much to say.

He said that an Irishwoman was waiting for his boat when they docked that morning – that they had come in early because the lines were freezing.

He said he forgot my number, but had recently been looking for me – admitted he called the Guggenheim Museum by mistake, even hung around the nightclub on weekends, watching people dance. Nobody knew who I was, he said.

He said his mother had been very sick when we met last summer on the bench at Gosman's Dock.

I asked if she was okay. He said she died.

Then a long silence that meant we were going to see each other.

When I went back to the meeting, the interns were looking through hundreds of World War II photographs for a proposed future exhibition. The photographs once belonged to American servicemen who were killed or went missing in Europe. They kept them in their wallets. They looked at them and wrote letters, maybe even held them as they died.

I thought of Grandpa John.

It's late afternoon in England. He's in the conservatory. It's raining. Soft thuds on the glass. My grandmother's steps keep him going. The memory of her steps keeps him going.

He's watering his plants.

Classical music is on.

During the war, he had a gun in someone's mouth. The man was trying to scream. A burst lip from the pushing metal. Eyes watering with fear and rage.

JOHN

FRANCE,

1944

I.

JOHN BRAY FELL silently through the night sky, his body less than it ever was, his life a collage devoid of single meaning.

The impact was so intense that John mistook his panic for death itself. Smoke and freezing air filled the cabin. The B-24 nosed into a dive. He formed a ladder with the syllables of his wife's name. Each syllable a rung closer to her, but further from God. A moment before jumping, John realized his leg was on fire and then a sudden freeze and darkness that meant he had made it. He tore at the harness, no time to count, he pulled at everything.

The navigator lived long enough to release his parachute, then fell without moving, a ring of stars in each eye. The others were captured or died from injuries soon after landing.

As the canopy spread and swung wildly, John feared for an instant that he was still attached to the aircraft. Then he looked around and saw nothing. He gripped the straps until his hands went numb. Breathing was quick and his lungs bled with cold. One of his feet was badly injured. A dense throb as though his heart had fallen into his boot.

He was still saying the word *Harriet* long after he'd forgotten he was doing it. Shaken loose from the association of memory, it was an awkward sound with no meaning.

He knew the enemy would find wings, the fuselage, bits of wire, a tail section, small fires.

He might never see Harriet again. They were married but had not yet lived together as man and wife. He might never see the diner where he grew up, or the street upon which he had played baseball and ridden his bicycle. He might never see the dog, or pet it on his way upstairs. He might never go out for ice cream on summer nights with his new wife in sandals, never stand in line at the post office, or ask to borrow the car. He would never stroll the boardwalk at Coney Island, and his dream of living with Harriet, kissing over tea at Lord & Taylor, dancing at the Palace, dizzy with happiness, would end before it had even begun.

His life was here now in the dark, in the emptiness, drifting through the air over Belgium or France.

It no longer mattered where.

Everything that happened to him from this moment on would be an encore.

JOHN

LONG ISLAND,

1939

II.

THE DINER WAS full of large parties. The air swirled in currents of smoke and laughter. Outside: Plymouths, Packards, and Fords held life in the haunches of their gleaming coats.

John clearing dishes. His mother's voice saying goodbye in the distance. The register and its tight bell. The smell of syrup. The fire of yolk over white plates. Uneaten crusts of toast. A single fork under the table. The ashtrays completely full. And somebody has forgotten a coat.

John lifted it from the back of the chair.

He or she would soon return with cold hands and the car running outside with the door open.

The coat was long with a belt. It was soft and possessed of a scent that seemed to lift him. It filled his body and was strongest on the collar. There were hairs, too, streaks of honey in waves upon the wool.

John took the coat into the staff room, and buried his face in the fabric. He held it against his body, to get an idea of her size. A name tag sewn below the collar spelled out her name, and like a vein, it pulsed beneath his fingers.

Harriet wasn't serious about John at first. He was three years younger and doted on her. But then after the attack on Pearl Harbor, she considered what her life would be like if he was sent to fight.

She harnessed the passion she had withheld and proposed marriage on a day trip to Montauk. It was what they both wanted. The sky was blue and cloudless. After lunch they watched seagulls. Fishing boats. Bristling lines of white frothed against the bow.

Across the ocean, Europe smouldered.

John found basic training difficult. It also hurt to be away. He couldn't do a lot of the things they wanted. He was told he would have to kill – would have to cross a field of guts to come home. John could tell that some of the others were ready, and it reassured him that one day he might be, too.

On Sundays he rode a bicycle into the countryside near the base, with a sketchbook and pencils. He sent Harriet his drawings of plants and never signed his letters. In the evenings he dressed and went into town in search of music. His superiors sometimes recognized him and waved from the orchestra section.

He stayed up late with the other men playing cards

and smoking cigarettes. He showed the picture of Harriet at Coney Island, and looked at it before bed. He never felt alone and always had someone to help when his weapon jammed during rifle practise.

John was well liked at home, too. His family had owned a diner for twenty-four years. He worked there after school for tips. He had a lifetime of stories. Pilots from Garden City would come in on their way back to Manhattan. Others drove for miles just to taste his mother's brisket.

The only fights John had in high school got as far as him being pushed over. He played clarinet in a band. He collected stamps and kept them in a shoe box.

His parents were quiet people. During the Depression, families they didn't recognize came in and ate quickly without talking. When the check arrived, it was always the same: fathers rifling through pockets for wallets that must have been dropped, lost, or even left in the pew at church.

John's parents always gave the same answer. 'Next time, then.' They figured it was going on all over the country, and had agreed never to humiliate a man in front of his children.

In the years following the Depression, John remembers his father calling him over to the counter from time to time as he sorted the day's mail. Sometimes the envelopes would include a letter, and once a photograph of a house with children standing in front of it. But mostly they just contained cheques for the exact amount of the meal, folded once, and with no return address.

John's father worked hard and listened to everything his wife said, even if he disagreed. He never raised his voice and liked to go to Mitchell Field to watch airplanes land.

The worst event of John's childhood was when his little cousin Jean got polio. She was taken away one morning and came back a year later in the body of an old woman.

JOHN

FRANCE,

1944

III.

IN THE DISTANCE, sudden flashes of light. The crackle of guns. John wondered where their B-24 had hit the ground. The flash of impact. He thought of his crew and tried to remember wives or mothers. He imagined a field of wreckage and the farmer for years to come, tripping on twists of charred metal. The pieces would sit in a bucket and outlive everyone involved.

He remembered that his pistol was still under the navigator's seat along with his wallet. Harriet would have rolled her eyes. 'Typical John.'

Then another shade of black that meant ground. He hit too soon to prepare and lost feeling in his injured foot. The ground was softer than he remembered at training because Europe is wetter.

John collected his billowing canopy and looked for a place to hide it. The sky glowed with dawn.

Then shapes appeared in the distance, dark figures approaching. He dropped his parachute and ran. Sharp pain forked up his torso; parts of his body dragged because he couldn't feel them. He ran for other shadows ahead, dense, motionless, ancient.

He imagined he was running for Harriet's coat in the forest before him. Leaves stuck to the wool, a hand appears, then arms, shoulders and the breathless climb to her neck. He would feel for the collar, then thread his life through the loops and hollows of her name.

The ground was thick with fallen leaves. If he could burrow, he had a chance. He must die and come back to life. He would recite the Bible, the Koran, the Talmud by simply declaring the name of someone he loved. He would trap the contents of his life in the safety of a single word, like a bubble in the sea.

Harriet was a young wife. She lay under sheets without moving.

Moonlight washed over her bed and chair.

The street outside was quiet, but the silence unbearable.

She could not feel the mud stuffed into John's mouth to prevent a fatal sneeze or cough, or the mess of shattered bones in his foot.

Instead she crept downstairs and built a large fire.

Her father woke to the snap of flames. He grabbed his robe and rushed out of the bedroom. The house glowed with the heat of his daughter's blaze, but he stopped halfway on the stairs, hypnotized by the flickering shadows and by the outline of his crying child.

He imagined the fighting overseas. The flashes and the cries. He could taste it in his mouth.

And as he stood there, not moving, his heart opened upon the many fields of dead, with their helmets on and their eyes pretending to see.

Love is also a violence, and cannot be undone.

MR HUGO

MANCHESTER, ENGLAND,

2010

I.

1948. WOKE UP screaming in a Paris hospital.

Soon after – sent to another ward where people walked around. Played games. Stared out the windows. Lay on the floor.

I learned to watch others for clues.

I had to watch, because I understood nothing.

I waited to eat. I waited for night.

Night came.

I waited for day.

First light.

Day.

I kept touching where my head should have been. I wanted to know why and understood nothing. I said nothing but watched all.

I nodded yes. I went along with all.

I was afraid and had nowhere else to go. I wondered about outside. I wondered from where I was.

Later on I was taken to the hospital garden. Amazed by wind. Wanted to be alone to watch people passing. There were so many people outside the hospital. I couldn't believe it. Thought we were the main ones.

Years passed. I started to understand what they

said. The same sounds over and over. I got used to them. I learned them and used them, too.

I spoke and understood some.

Paris liberated seven years ago, they said.

Everyone had a story. Nurse just a girl, father tortured.

I had been shot in the face, they said, and showed pictures of me in a magazine:

UN MYSTÉRIEUX PARISIEN CONTINUE DE DÉFIER LA MORT!

Years tossed things upon the shore. Souvenirs of what was.

Knew the faces of those I had slaughtered but said nothing. You have to understand that I was one of *those*: hated.

I remember the grey sleeves. Could feel the weight of a rifle. The helmets got cool at night. Buildings on fire. Flames drowned out the screaming. Watching calmly as a man scoops up the remains of his child with such gentleness we thought she was asleep.

There was a time before when I was a boy.

One memory is of a man with ropes in his hands, bumps of hot soup against my lips, then the bowl crashing to the kitchen floor. Soup fills the cracks beneath. Pieces of the broken bowl like teeth.

Father maybe.

Another memory is an open door. The smell of mud. Delicate, wet feet. Bare feet. A woman is outside. An open door. Mud. A woman is out there. Buried. Find her, I'm telling myself, *find her.* But it's a dream.

Mother maybe.

It took years to speak again. My French was not perfect. But any sound was a miracle.

It wasn't an easy life in there, but not bad. Other patients kept me company, and there were always others coming and going. Some liked talking. Some lay on the floor and wouldn't get up. Some smashed their heads against the wall so there was blood. Then nurses running. A struggle. Injection anywhere. Carried away in sleep.

One day they said I had to go. I packed a bag with my clothes, shoes, and soap. My name was written on the case (in case).

Driven to Gare du Nord. Sat in Gare du Nord. Slept in Gare du Nord. Beaten in Gare du Nord.

I found petrified bread in the bins and drank from a tap. Mostly I sat watching. The clap of the timetable. Even at night, in darkness, the applause of letters falling.

I slept under newspapers. Hid in the stories of others.

At night, I watched distant lights grow into bright eyes. Trains approaching. Then in summer, there were tourists and the gendarmes made us leave. I went outside and lived on the streets then. No more applause. No more beating. No more wet platforms or bright eyes.

Outside was okay. There were so many others. The sky very open. Unlimited breathing, I thought.

I used to watch the river. A cool muscle. There were always boats in the rippling with music inside. People dancing. No sound except rushing. I couldn't see the river at night but heard it. Couples walked along its banks. The rhythm of shoes. Chains of lamplight flickering on the water.

Also, the sound of laughter. Children up late, pointing, shouting back to their parents, then running, not away but deeper: happiness, not fear.

People were always staring, of course. You can imagine. Who can blame them? Half a man's head is missing. From one side I looked normal. Like before but with no memory of before. Then I, Mr Hugo, turn my head, people gasp. Afraid of what is *not there.* From the front my eyes look okay, my neck looks fine – but then suddenly half a head is missing, and did I mention that I have only one ear?

I didn't mind sitting. I got numb, but it was quiet. I waited for night. Night came. I fought to keep warm. With the armour of dawn came relief. I watched day unfold from inside, then slept where sunlight pooled.

Anyone who is desperate or alone will agree there is comfort in routine.

I hit the usual benches, boulevards. Notre Dame. The cinemas were safe for sleeping if you didn't get caught. Parks were safe, too, if others joined. There was one park we all knew, where a small boy, a baker's boy, came running (young thief), with a sack of croissants, chocolate buns, bread, tarts, whatever he grabbed. We gobbled. Always gave me extra, and didn't mind my head. Ate fast, we all did – despite the agony of teeth.

I liked mornings there. I felt light. I glanced up even – to Him. I talked quietly to Him. I felt Him listening. *Lost my way*, I told Him. But He knows. Was there when it happened.

I started to stop at every church. I hunched below coloured windows, and drowned in stories of mankind. Some faces drawn in the glass had small but powerful eyes. Sometimes a priest would come and sit with me, talk to me, touch my hand. It felt nice. I wondered if His hand touches all, or if ours touch His. I remembered then, books in an attic. Small hands. Forbidden but they crawled through boxes anyway. Boxes of books and other boxes. Then I thought of the boy who brings cakes to the park for us. I wanted to boast to the priest. I felt proud to know someone like that, he knows Him, but I know Someone, too. A child with the power to save us.

There were always men beside the river. In summer we were there all night. Some had red faces and staggered when they stood. I was offered drink and something to smoke. But it wasn't allowed at the hospital, so I wasn't used to it. It was the right idea sitting under bridges, though. There were many shady places away from the crowd. It was cool in summer, with my back against the stone. I didn't mind being alone. I watched all. I listened. Slept. Felt okay if I never woke up.

Sleeping under the Pont des Arts one day. A doctor from the hospital out with her kids noticed me sleeping (knew my head of course). She was shocked to see Mr Hugo.

She drove me back to the hospital. There was lots of pointing and raised voices.

The chief visited the next day. He said he needed a

caretaker. I would live in another part of the hospital near the attic. It was the perfect solution, he said, and gave me money for new clothes, soap, a comb, shoelaces, even. I lived in the old part, above wards that were closed in 1890. There were many empty rooms. Most were locked.

I was maybe in my thirties then. At least young enough to still dream of what I would never have.

I spent free time in the parks, sometimes recognizing an old face – I was happy to share lunch, I wanted to, even, and brought more.

I often went to the library. I was reading by then. I read a lot. I liked poetry. I read it in French. I learned some English too. Great escapes. I will admit I knew what German was, had the sounds in my head, like eggs ready to hatch when I heard it spoken in the street. Those sounds belonged to me, yet I had no memory of them. I felt dread when I heard it, shame, even. I went home after and defecated on myself. I sat there in the smell. I made myself. I made myself sit there in the smell. I was one of those, remember – one of those: *hated.*

Anyway, as a caretaker I woke up at 5:00 a.m. Beyond each pane were the outlines of things coming – a world drawn fresh from the memory of yesterday.

My job started at 6:00 a.m. I wore blue overalls. I had a heavy key. There was a cupboard of mops, brushes, and basic tools. There were insects living in the cupboard, but they were there before me, so I tried not to disturb them.

I shared ideas with the people who came. They were not all idiots and criminals; there were intelligent ones too, respected men and women with jobs and homes, families who would visit and sob quietly.

Patients came and went. Some escaped and left their bodies behind. I thought I'd die in there too, and I wanted to, mostly in the evening.

Yet here I am, years later, between this page and your eye. Part of someone else's story.

After nineteen years, the hospital closed down. The same chief came to see me. He was a widower by then and about to retire. His children had grown too. I have to admit we were used to each other.

He made phone calls for me. *Would arrange things*, he said. There was a caretaker position at the Manchester Royal Infirmary in England. *Same job*, he said. *Room to grow, even.*

He drove me in his car to England.

It took two days. We had to share a bed in a small hotel.

He talked about his wife. Cried. I listened to all. I watched all through the car window. When we got there, he helped me find a place to live.

It had taken months to get a passport.

The authorities said I didn't exist. There was only one official document: the hospital admission form for an unidentified male with a rifle wound to the head. Former hospital staff were telephoned. But there were so many injured. Most died.

Then an old woman who once worked in the kitchen said she could faintly recall: *Left to die in the street*, she said. *Without any identification, rags for clothes, pockets empty except for a novel by Victor Hugo. It was the admitting doctor's idea for a name. Didn't think I'd live.*

I had to go down to the passport office with the chief. I had to show what was left of my face.

They stopped what they were doing.

Was a victim of war, he explained, *no first name known*, he said. *No last name known*, he said. *Exceptions had to be made.*

Exceptions were made. Passport: Victor Hugo. Born Paris 1922. Number: 88140175.

The English streets are dark and grey. It's hard to understand what people are saying.

And the damp!

I learned to take hot baths before bed.

Three major things happened in the decades after Paris:

1. I joined a monthly poetry group.
2. I became friends with a boy who moved in next door for a few years.
3. I built a greenhouse for the cultivating of tomatoes.

One day I was told I had to retire. Why? I asked.

Laughed, they all did. Told me was time to enjoy my life. There was a small party. People who didn't know me got drunk. I sat down. I watched all. Listened. Wondered if He could see.

I spoke English well by then. But still they looked, still they pitied, still they feared and sometimes spat.

And life kept going . . . kept dragging me along in its teeth.

A man came to see me last month at the house. At first I wouldn't let him in. Then he told me he worked at the BBC. I wondered if I was watching too much. *Had a friend in America*, he said. *Asked if he would deliver a letter to an old neighbour called Mr Hugo.*

It was something I had been too afraid to wish for. Some days I wondered if I had imagined him.

He told me to read the letter. Think it over. He would come back in a couple of weeks and help make arrangements if it was something I wanted. He told me to consider the next few years. He asked if I would get lonely. (I laughed at that one.)

He said California is always sunny. He said Danny is a famous director now and his films are shown all over the world. *Would be a nice place to spend time*, he said. *The retirement centre even has a pool and small garden.*

I asked him to stay for dinner and cooked fish fingers. He arranged french fries in the oven dish. I put on children's programmes. We watched and ate off trays. It got late. He touched my hand before he left. I gave him tomatoes.

Went to bed. Lay awake with my eyes open. Would have to leave my home. Would have to leave my poetry group – would not catch the bus twice a month on Tuesday, would not sit at the back and read names and messages scratched into the glass. Would not know that:

Daz luvz Raz
Gareth is a Twat
Lizzie is a slag

Declarations of love or anger.
To think:
Most fought until the end,
Murdered until the end,
Hated until the end.

And I was one of those, remember – one of those: *hated.*

I should tell Danny. He has a right to know what Mr Hugo did.

On nights when the poetry group meets, I boil an egg in the kettle. I take it with me on the bus. It keeps my hands warm until eaten. Sometimes I take a bag of tomatoes that I cultivated in the greenhouse and give them out. I will miss all that. I am attached to things most people find insignificant.

I will miss this house and the birds outside every morning. Just open your window at dawn and you'll understand. People who sleep through it wake to silence.

New people in the poetry group always want to know where I lived when I was a boy. *Far away*, I tell them. They think I'm wise – think I have a story. But the older I get, the less I understand.

So I make things up. *The smell of hay. Falling asleep under trees. Riding a bicycle across an entire country, picking vegetables in a field.* No point going on about the starvation, or father's fists, or the ropes and how much I screamed – not so much for pain but because I loved him, and wanted our lives to be different.

Though it *is* true I grew up in an old blacksmith's cottage. *Best place to live in winter,* I always add, *as the fireplace is larger than normal.*

Inside, I go on, *a stone floor worn down in one place. It's where horses stood. A shoe is being fitted. A horse's leg has to be lifted with strength and gentleness.*

Outside, cows tearing across hillsides.

Probably 1938.

My father convinced the men in town I was older than I was.

Thought he was helping me.

He said, *When you come back, a kiss for every Jew.*

JOHN

FRANCE,

1944

I.

JOHN AWOKE IN a stew of mud and dead leaves with a fierce pain in his foot. His wristwatch had stopped a few minutes before nine.

He expected the enemy would return with more men or dogs, and so untangled himself quickly from the bush.

Here was a landscape John had always loved. Roots poked up through the ground on their way to deeper earth. Heavy mosses wrapped dead branches and smoothed the gnarls of dying trunks. It was an old wood that had seen many wars, and once even hosted a gang of deserters from Napoleon's Grande Armée, whose uniforms and weapons were still tucked into the hollow of a dead tree.

Harriet had several sketchbooks of John's drawings. They were lush and messy. She liked to look at them. Over the course of their lives, she hoped he might teach her how to draw. It could be something they did together, a way to fill the Sundays ahead.

John's escape from this place would have to be a work of art, something original, something the enemy would not anticipate.

He stepped slowly through the forest, trying not to break small branches underfoot, when two arms grabbed him from behind. He struggled and kicked his legs violently, but the person holding him was much bigger. A voice told him to relax, and he did. The thick arms loosened.

The man wore a long waterproof coat with tall farmer's boots.

'I knew you were here somewhere,' the man said with a French accent. 'We saw you land, but you fled before we could get to you.'

The farmer led John through the woods to a pile of potatoes at the edge of a plowed field. There was also a cart and a muscular horse that looked up when they approached. Pheasants were penned in a wire basket and pressed their feathered bodies against the mesh.

The man told John that his cousin's farm was on the other side of the village, and that's where they were going. John watched as he filled several sacks with potatoes and then hauled them onto the cart.

When the farmer picked up the final sack, he motioned for John to get in. Then he filled it with a few handfuls of potatoes and stacked it against the others.

After a jerk, they began to move. A short time later

there was a sudden echo of hooves, and John realized they had left the field for a road. The pheasants were flapping against the sides of the basket. John closed his eyes and tried to block the pain in his foot, but it was hard to keep still.

When the cart stopped, men spoke quickly in German. The farmer said in French, 'Come and see what I found.'

The soldiers stopped talking and followed him.

After the farmer had presented the pheasants to the soldiers, John heard matches being struck. The odour of cigarette smoke. Nobody talking.

His foot stung so wildly that he felt in danger of being betrayed by his own body. Just as he began to stir, there was a great weight on the cart, and John felt a large back lean against him.

When they reached the house, John was carried inside and released from the sack. The farmer's name was Paul. He had witnessed the invasion from the fields. The sky full of parachutes. Equipment stuck in the mud, wheels spinning. The rattle of machine guns upon anyone who resisted. Paul said that people he once trusted were profiteering from others' misery, or openly walking with soldiers in the square, out of fear or for advancement. He attended the public executions of his friends, helped bury them afterward, and listened to the stories of soldiers sneaking out of their barracks in search of girls they had seen. Nobody was safe, he said.

He told John other things too, about his horses and the weather.

How high the river was.

He gave his American guest hot coffee, and asked how he would like his potatoes cooked. John thanked him and rolled up his sleeves to help, but had to sit because of his foot.

In between mouthfuls, John confessed how he didn't consider himself much of a killer. Paul nodded. 'We all felt that way at the beginning,' he said. 'Probably even a few of them did too, but now it's too late.'

When Paul questioned him about his crew, John told him they were dead and then changed the subject.

John was part of Operation Carpetbagger. They had taken off at 23:12 from RAF Harrington. His B-24 Liberator was called the *Starduster.* His best friend was Leo Arlin from Brooklyn, who flew with another crew. The B-24 bombers had been adapted for special operations, and painted black.

It was safer if Paul knew nothing – even if he was a member of the Maquis.*

---

* Members of the French Resistance from rural areas.

John had met many French agents. Part of Operation Carpetbagger meant placing the right person in the right place at the right time. The best operative had no name and no family. Most went missing. Fates remained a mystery. Some agents carried cyanide capsules. If capture seemed imminent, death would take only a few moments.

Captured agents were tortured, then shot or decapitated. Known relatives could face a similar fate, regardless of age. John considered these things as he stared at the toy box and family of dolls set up for a tea party on the floor.

Paul's cousin's clothes were too big for John, but Paul said the sleeves and trousers could be hemmed. The clothes were also a little damp, so Paul hung them in the kitchen above the stove.

As John put more wood on the fire, Paul went outside and returned with a metal bathtub. A pair of heavy arms swung out from the fireplace, with hooks for Paul to hang pots of water. When the water was hot, Paul lifted the pots with a rag, and poured them into the tub.

As John undressed, they were both surprised at the state of his foot. After the bath, Paul gave John some rope to bite on while he cleaned the wound.

As Paul delicately wrapped the swollen joint, John asked what time his cousin and family would be home. When the bandage was snug, Paul gave John a stick to lean on and led him outside.

The cool air felt good and the sky was full of stars.

Beyond the farmhouse was a line of low huts where the chickens slept. John wondered what Paul wanted to show him. It was painful to walk and he was worried about being seen.

When they reached a cluster of young fruit trees, Paul stopped. John was about to say something when he looked down and saw four mounds of earth, all faintly indented with handprints. Each was marked with a different-sized cross.

Paul leaned down and touched the smallest one.

'Jacqui was only three,' he said. 'But it made no difference.'

Until further notice, John was to spend daylight hours in the cellar. Paul would bring him upstairs at night after curfew, to eat by the fire and talk or play cards.

The cellar smelled like wet magazines. John composed letters to Harriet in his mind. He relived their trip to Coney Island, the gust of wind that blew off his hat, the fishing boats at Montauk, the feeling of her hand inside his.

Paul supplied John with painkillers that made him tired and dreamy. The sound of water through the drainpipe filled him with awe. Heavy showers of rain like music.

They spent most nights beside the fire in silence. Paul often fell asleep because he was farming his cousin's land in addition to his own.

John grew a beard, as Paul said a mustache would have made him look too English. He also found John a good pair of shoes that fit well.

The days passed, and John's health deteriorated. Paul took care of his foot as best he could, but it was changing colour. Paul studied it by the fire one night and said he'd try to find a doctor. John had grown dependent on the painkillers. Paul showed him where they were, in case something happened to him.

The next morning John heard the latch and thought it was the doctor. A voice called his name, then a single match was struck to light a candle. A face appeared in the entrance to the cellar, and a hand motioned for John to come upstairs. When John hesitated, an old man climbed down the steps with the candle balanced in one hand. He approached John cautiously, then handed him a revolver.

'You can trust me,' he said.

They sat in the kitchen and drank coffee. The

wallpaper was yellow and worn out around the light switch. The old man fed John some pâté and a crust of bread that he brought wrapped in a tea towel. He was the town mayor, and said that Paul was trying to find a doctor – but it was hard to trust anyone.

'Your foot might be the end of us all,' he laughed.

Then he loaded the stove stick by stick. When the wood basket was empty, the old man began picking up the toys that littered the floor. John got up to help.

'He'll be angry at first,' the mayor said. 'But it's for his own good.'

Some of the dolls were sticky. Smiles had been drawn on with crayon.

When Paul didn't return that night, John packed a few things and left quietly through the back door.

Days had turned into weeks.

It was dark and the streets of the village were empty. This made the main patrol easier to evade.

Some houses had been burned, and there was black around the window frames like smudges of mascara.

When a dog started barking, John looked down a side street and saw a small group of soldiers marching towards him. They would want to check his papers – especially as it was past curfew.

If he ran, they would notice and give chase.

He stood still for a moment, then spotted a light on in a shop up ahead. He walked briskly towards it and entered without hesitating. A bell sounded. It was a barbershop. A solemn-faced man appeared from the back and stood with a towel. He ushered John into a chair and began brushing his face with foam from a large bowl. The patrol passed to the aroma of lavender and vetiver.

After splashing on some aftershave, the barber went downstairs and reappeared with a heavy coat. In the pockets were bread rolls, dried meat, money, a compass, and a small comb.

John left the village at exactly ten o'clock (if the local church was to be believed), and set the wristwatch Harriet had given him for his birthday. Soon he was crawling through hedgerows and skirting the edges of fields.

He darted across roads as quickly as he could, but on one occasion found himself caught in the lamps of a motorcycle and sidecar. It had stopped some distance away with its engine off, at the front of a convoy of troop carriers.

John pretended to be drunk, but nothing happened. Either the soldiers hadn't seen him or they were amused. John fumbled to undo his belt, then urinated in the road.

It was long past curfew. They could take him in or just gun him down, depending on how busy they were. When he finished, John buttoned up his trousers and staggered beyond the arc of the motorcycle's headlamps and into the safety of a field. He lay down some distance away and watched the convoy for a few moments, then he swallowed two painkillers and set off again quickly.

His plan was to go north, where he hoped to find passage on a boat to England or make contact with the Maquis.

He walked until the first glow of dawn. His clothes were wet from dew. While searching for somewhere to shelter, he heard two bombers hedgehopping at low altitude and wondered if they were from Harrington, and whether he knew the crew. The Carpetbaggers flew only when there was enough moon to navigate by rivers and lakes.

News would have reached Harriet and his parents some time ago. He imagined them at the kitchen table trying to get used to the idea. A hush over the restaurant that would last decades. Sadness in the kitchen, and in the cake tins, and on the plates with the eggs and hash browns.

When John came upon a derelict cottage, he went in because the sun was beginning to rise. The floor was covered with cans and broken glass. Stale, dank air was heavy with the stench of urine. There was an enormous hole in the roof where a shell had entered, and continued through the floor into the cellar. A steady dripping and the echo of drops told John the cellar was flooded. He took off his coat and lit a candle. At first it was difficult to see, but he held the candle as low as he could into the hole. The cellar was also a garage, and against the far wall was the outline of a car. There were also wooden beams, splintered furniture, broken crockery, and what appeared to be the white glow of a human body. John backed away and looked for a place to lie down.

He woke twelve hours later at dusk and lay still, trying to make sense of what was happening. In the silence, he could hear his own heart thudding along – as if counting down the time he had left to live.

Before continuing on his journey, John decided to brave the cellar. He first checked for any sign of life outside, then removed his shoes, socks, and bandages. After rolling up his trousers, he dropped a few large pieces of furniture through the hole, wincing at the clatter. Then he climbed down slowly. The icy water numbed the pain in his foot. His plan was to open the hood of the car and get some tubing that would be useful for breathing underwater.

The hood of the car creaked so loudly that John felt certain anyone outside would have heard. For a few moments he listened, but could hear only his breath and the faint whistle of morning wind through the ruins.

The engine and chassis had already begun to rust. John melted wax onto the fender as a base for his candle and located the hose he wanted. It came out easily, and he climbed back up using the stack of furniture, making sure not to disturb the remains of the previous tenant.

After packing up, John wound his watch and went outside. It was almost completely dark. He crept around the house looking for food, and located a small patch of carrots growing near a heavy-leafed vegetable that had mostly been eaten by slugs.

After taking more painkillers, he continued north, skirting villages and scrambling for cover at the faintest murmur of an engine. There was a great deal of action in the air, and John lay on his back sometime around midnight to watch a brilliant firefight.

His plan was proving to be a success, and he considered that he might try to reach an even more northerly position on the coast.

When dawn came, it was dry and warm. With no buildings in sight, John squeezed his body into a hedge, and spread his limbs around the branches and roots, the same way he had hidden himself that first night. He urinated by turning his body to the side (defecating only on the move – so the smell wouldn't draw attention from anyone passing).

Despite eating half of the food he was carrying, John fell asleep very hungry, then woke about ten hours later in the early evening with no appetite at all. He also felt dizzy, and his foot was so bad that he was half tempted to put a bullet in it himself.

When it was dark enough to travel again, John pulled himself out of the hedge for a third night of walking. For the first hour, he had to vomit several times. Then his stomach seemed to dry out and settle.

The landscape changed. Fields churned by fighting and low fences of barbed wire. John wondered if, by some miracle, he had reached the Belgian border. Then it started raining, and he felt very sick. When dawn came he lay under a tree and passed out.

Nine hours later, when faced with a fourth night of walking, John considered that he wasn't going to make it.

If he gave himself up, he would be tortured and killed; if he pushed on, he would certainly collapse. He also convinced himself that he'd been walking in circles, and that Paul's farm was only a few hundred yards away. With the help of four painkillers he kept going. There were rain showers all night, and by dawn John was soaked through and barely able to take a step. His forehead burned with fever and his vision was blurred.

Sometime in the early hours of the morning, he looked around and realized he was surrounded by human remains. He fumbled for his pistol and cocked the hammer. Muddied uniforms of German infantry torn to shreds. They had been attacked from the air with machine guns.

Then John saw a cat. He tried to follow it in the hope it would lead him to a farmhouse, but it turned out to be a helmet filled with mud. He fell on his knees and stared at the helmet, realizing that it was not mud after all.

An hour or so later, John opened his eyes to the growl of a tank. There were no trees or hedgerows in which to take cover, so he rolled into a deep tank track. His intention was to blend in with the other corpses in the field.

As he shifted his limbs in the mud, John realized

there was a body beneath his, and when it moved, John flipped over and rammed his pistol into a steadily opening mouth. Two eyes, white with panic, stared at him. John gripped the trigger and waited for the tank to get closer. The noise would mask the shot.

DANNY

LOS ANGELES,

2009

L

I.

Danny hummed Bach partitas on the freeway and thought of the pianist Glenn Gould in a heavy coat. He knew very little about his father, and often thought of him too.

Some days the sky was so clear, it was like staring into darkness.

Danny moved to Los Angeles from Scotland in his late twenties, determined to be a success, determined to direct pictures his way, and to make life easy for his mother in her old age.

He was born in Manchester, England, and often imagined the moment of his delivery. Screaming for sure, hard fluorescent light, his mother's shaking hands and glistening forehead, white towels on the floor, nurses in starched uniforms with steel watches pinned to their aprons. In her arms, nothing could hurt him.

When Danny was only a week old, his father taped a note to the television to say he would never come back.

Danny's mother went from job to job. She was always late for work because it was hard to find people she could trust with her son. Her parents lived in London. Her father wanted to move back to Nigeria, but her mother was happier in Britain. They invited her to come and live with them, but Danny's mother couldn't imagine being in her old bedroom with a baby.

When Danny was about twelve years old, his mother fell in love and they left Manchester for Scotland.

The marriage ended after two years with more relief than resentment. His mother battled her disappointment in private, and enrolled in night school to study sociology and nursing. Danny used to walk home from school, then let himself in and watch television until his mother got back and started dinner.

She had a few friends, but liked most of all to be at home with her son.

The block of flats where they lived overlooked a supermarket. There was also a canal guarded by a tall fence. Holes had been opened in the wire, and the fence resembled a spider's web teased apart by children with twigs. On the grassy descent to the murky water, there were car tires, a mattress, oil cans, and a ripped armchair that lay upside down. Pupils from a local comprehensive often bought lunches at the supermarket, then ate them noisily on a grass verge above metal lines of shopping trolleys.

Rubbish blew against the fence and formed piles.

In summer, the upside-down armchair, the car tires, mattress, and other discarded items disappeared under tall, lush weeds.

After Danny moved across town into a flat of his own, he visited his mother several evenings a week – and always on Sunday, with a small box of Milk Tray chocolates to eat during *Songs of Praise*. She knew each chocolate by its shape. Danny liked the hard caramels because they lasted.

He stayed until she went to bed, then called a minicab and waited inside until it came. The flats were not as safe as they once had been. Gangs of teenage boys shouted things and followed at a distance.

When Danny mentioned that he was thinking of moving to Los Angeles, his mother could tell it was what he wanted.

She came to Glasgow International Airport, and watched him inch along the security line. He knew he would never come back to live in Scotland and felt the pull of another home that could never truly be his.

Danny's employment in Los Angeles was prearranged to satisfy immigration requirements. He had already worked in television for years. Starting immediately after college, he made coffee and ran errands.

There were others his age, but Danny was the only intern who put chocolates on the saucers, and left notes for the actors to say how well they had done. After a few years on set, he instinctively knew where the couch should be for the murder sequence, and how the detective should enter the pub, and for how long he should stand at the bar before having a heart attack, and whether glasses should break or not in his fall, and who should scream (and how).

By twenty-five he was doing well, but for Danny it was not enough. Instead of joining the others at the pub after a hard day of shooting, he went back to his small flat and read Shakespeare, Beckett, Artaud, and Ibsen – studied Cassavetes, Antonioni, Ozu, and Bergman.

After directing a few short pieces for BBC Two, Danny started writing his own scripts. There were so many techniques that interested him. Ideas flickered like small fires.

The first four years in Los Angeles were not easy. Americans work day and night. His first film took a long time to make but everyone was satisfied. His second was quiet but allowed him to pay his debts. His third picture, an historical drama about the Resistance called *Ste. Anne's Night*, was nominated for an Academy Award in the category of Best Director, but

Danny felt the film didn't work, and needed to make a fourth to find out why.

About that time he bought his mother a modern flat in the Quayside section of Glasgow. He flew back to Scotland for a week and they shopped for furniture. She kept saying, 'You don't have to, Danny, you really shouldn't.'

It took her six months to settle in. She would sometimes walk around the flat at night and touch things. Danny called twice a week, and they talked for about an hour.

During preproduction on his fourth film, Danny moved from the Silver Lake section of Los Angeles to the Hollywood Hills. He traded his El Camino for a white Mercedes with tan leather, and hired someone to shout at him regularly in the gym. On the backseat of his car was a Scottish wool blanket for his three beagles. His mother had sent it with a six-month supply of tea bags, and some HP sauce.

Ten years passed.

His mother retired. The beagles were slower and howled less. There were grey hairs on their noses. Danny enjoyed listening to music in the car and being at home with his dogs. He liked sometimes to swim, then eat his breakfast outside with *The New*

York Times. Bougainvillea and jasmine grew around the pool, and there were many birds.

When Danny needed to think, he drove all night through the desert to Las Vegas, stopping to fill his mouth with warm air and to scoop up handfuls of sand. After living in Scotland for so long, it had taken years to warm up. He stopped for meals at roadside diners, chatted with the waitresses, and watched people play Lotto machines, drink coffee, smoke quietly, and sweep the pay phones for coins. There were sometimes showers for truck drivers. You could see them in a line at the counter with wet hair, eating eggs.

Danny's office took up a suite at Soho House – a Hollywood hotel and members-only club. The management was British, and there were items on the menu like fish and chips, and mushy peas. He could host parties without leaving the building, and sit alone on the balcony when it rained. A waiter once sat with him during a heavy shower. He was from Galway, and also felt the pull of a home he would never return to.

Tell them that we need them to go up to five,' Danny said. Other lines flashed but were taken by his secretary.

He opened the top drawer of his desk.

'I just looked for cigarettes,' he said. 'Can you believe it?'

He took an unsharpened pencil and rolled it in his mouth.

'No, not for a month now.'

He swivelled in his chair to face the city outside his window.

'It's a pencil, I swear,' Danny said. 'Anyway, I'm doing it for the dogs, not myself.' He listened for a moment. 'Tell Stan that we appreciate his enthusiasm, actually no, that's patronizing – tell him we appreciate the relationship we have with him, but can't move forward for less than what they paid before – but then they already know this; it's just what they do, you know that.'

He listened again. 'All right, do that then – as long as it's in the contract, it will cost them more in the long run, but if it makes him look good, it's fine – if you think it's a good move. I trust your judgment.'

He nodded, and wrote a few things down.

'Before you go, Jack,' Danny said, 'I was planning to stop by and see Raquel this afternoon. Let her know for me, would you?'

It was very hot outside and there were no clouds.

The sign in the distance once read HOLLYWOODLAND. Mules hauled thick poles up the steep ravine for mounting the letters. In 1932, an actress jumped to her death from the letter H. There were old-style cars parked along the boulevards. Men wore hats and beige suits. Everybody smoked and rode horses. The writer F. Scott Fitzgerald ate at lunch counters, and sat in a park near the tar pits, writing letters to his daughter, telling her not to spend so much money and to look after her mother.

Danny's secretary, Preston, knocked and came in. He was from Youngstown, Ohio. His first job was at a popular brunch place in Echo Park. He wore bow ties. He went to a lot of parties. He called his parents every Sunday when they got home from church. They were encouraging but wanted him back in Ohio. His mother wore slippers with fluff inside. She liked to put her feet up when she watched television. Preston's father coloured her hair once a month. He wore plastic gloves and the kitchen smelled of chemicals. They were both forty years old when he was born. It was their wedding anniversary last week. They had a barbeque with ribs, fried chicken, okra, corn bread, collard greens, and homemade pork and beans. Preston's father e-mailed pictures. People ate off paper plates and held up Dixie cups to the camera.

Nobody cared when they found out Preston was gay. He told his parents one Sunday night with the television on. He told them it was as natural as breathing.

How's the Paramount thing, Preston?' Danny asked without looking up.

'Great, that new producer is like a Christmas miracle, I should have something for you by tomorrow.'

'And are you going home for Christmas, Preston?'

'Yes, if you don't mind. Are you going to Scotland?'

'Actually Mum's coming here – though I think she's more excited about seeing the dogs.'

'It's much warmer here than Scotland, right?'

'It's warmer everywhere, Preston. Do you need anything else from me?'

'No, I should have something for you to look at tomorrow.'

'Okay. I'm going to see Jack's wife this afternoon – would you call the hospital and make sure everything is fine, ask the nurse if she needs anything?'

'How is she?'

'Probably bored more than anything.'

'I've got some magazines on my desk if you want to take them?'

'I'm glad you have time to read magazines, Preston.'

The parking garage was bright and always busy. An automatic chime sounded until Danny attached his seat belt. 'Thanks, Grandma,' he said.

There was a rubber bone on the passenger seat, and a dent in the driver's-side door that the Soho House parking attendants were always offering to have repaired while Danny was upstairs in his office.

Occasionally he would insist on parking the car himself and then recline the front seat all the way back for a nap.

He often daydreamed of childhood and the rain-swept terraced house in Manchester where he grew up with his mother. He thought of her often, because he was old enough to understand things, old enough to remember when she was the age he is now. She had loved him but withheld herself from others. The mark of her life was not only what she had done, but what she had denied herself.

Danny felt they were similar. He preferred to be at home with his beagles and a cup of tea. There were so many parties and dinners that they didn't mean anything anymore. He no longer felt the need to convince anyone of anything. Everything he found interesting went into his films and he had nothing else to say. He had enjoyed a few light relationships over the years, but the men he was attracted to always wanted more than he was willing to give.

He would not have described himself as lonely, but *would* have admitted that something was missing. He often sat at his kitchen counter wondering what it could be, watching his dogs sleep, watching them breathe, their small hearts turning and opening like locks.

II.

BEFORE JOINING THE freeway that would take him to the hospital, Danny stopped at Lucques on Melrose to buy a package of homemade cookies for Raquel. It was early, and the owner, Jane, was doing paperwork at the end of the bar.

'Not staying for lunch, Dan?'

'No, I'm going to visit a friend in hospital – Jack Miller's wife.'

'Oh, I know who you're talking about – Jack and Raquel. I can picture her. I hope it's nothing serious.'

'She'll be in very soon for lunch, by which time, Jane – you'll have forgotten this conversation.'

'She doesn't want anyone to know she's in the hospital?'

'Who knows,' Danny said.

'Jesus, you're discreet,' Jane said. 'Remind me to tell you my secrets sometime.'

'Preston doesn't call me the Vault for nothing, you know.'

When Danny got back to his car, the meter had expired, but there was no ticket on the windshield. In the bag, he found a few extra cookies packed separately from the box. He put three in his pocket for when he got home, then ate the fourth standing up. Opposite the restaurant was a shop that sold vintage watches. Danny looked at them in the window. Such tiny lines and numbers, such delicate springs, all hard at work on something they would never understand.

Raquel had been sick for months. Her hair fell out during the treatments, but the worst was over, she said.

When Danny arrived at the hospital, he asked the valet if he could park the car himself. It was a peculiar habit of his that people in Los Angeles didn't understand. One valet accused him of not trusting Spanish people. Danny was so offended that he got out of the car and kicked a small dent in the door with the heel of his shoe, but they just thought he was crazy.

When he got to the main desk, there were five women pointing people in various directions and placing others on hold with their long nails.

'Hello, sir, how can I help you?'

'I'm not sure I'm in the right part – '

'Give me the name of the patient, sir, and I'll look them up in the system.'

'Crane with a C, and Raquel is her first name.'

The woman made a few strokes on her keyboard.

'Mrs Crane, Raquel Crane. Are you Mr Crane?'

'No, I'm Uncle Crane.'

'I beg your pardon?'

'I'm just a close friend . . . no blood relation.'

'You need Oncology, Building O-Fourteen. Just go out these doors and take a right and look for the letter O building – or you can take the elevator here and there's a floating bridge that will connect you. If you get lost, pick up any phone and dial zero.'

'Thank you,' Danny said.

'I hope your friend feels better.'

Raquel's ward had its own private receptionist. There were vases of flowers on her desk, and balloons. One of the balloons had come untethered and touched the ceiling at a slight bend. The receptionist walked Danny along the hall. She offered to carry the magazines and cookies he had stuffed into a tote bag that read FOX SEARCHLIGHT PICTURES.

Raquel was sleeping.

Her room was bright and luxurious. He stood by the window and looked out at Los Angeles in the distance. An endless stream of cars surged like colourful dots through the canyon. Traffic helicopters hovered over Sunset Boulevard. Danny quietly typed a message to Preston asking him to make sure insurance was covering Raquel's room.

Then he sat in a beige leather chair beside the sleeping woman who had brought an immeasurable amount of happiness to his life. She had been married to his agent and best friend for seven years. They were trying for a child when the doctor found a lump.

Danny took out the magazines and looked at the faces on the covers. Everyone was searching, he thought – trying to unravel the knot of their lives.

When Raquel woke up, she reached for his hand.

'Why aren't you on set doing something amazing?' she asked quietly.

'I prefer nursing.'

'I think Jack does too,' Raquel said, and sat up.

'I like your hair.'

Raquel giggled and fingered the thick strands. 'It's a wig.'

'You can't tell.'

She blushed. 'It's bad enough not being allowed make-up.'

Danny squeezed her hand. 'I spoke to Jack this morning.'

'I know,' she said. 'He called to say you were coming.' She paused for a moment. 'When *he* came yesterday, he couldn't stop crying. Did he mention anything?'

Danny shook his head.

'Don't tell him I told you.'

Jack had always seemed confident about what was going to happen, even taking classes on the process of treatment and joining an online support group.

'Keep an eye on him for me, Danny.'

'I will,' he promised, searching her face for some sign of what was to come. She pointed to the magazines on her bedside table.

'Are those for me?'

Danny read the titles. 'French *Vogue,* Italian *Vogue,* British *Vogue,* Chinese *Elle, World of Interiors, Hello, OK,* and *Tatler.*'

Raquel laughed, but it seemed painful somehow. 'Thank Preston for me, would you, Danny? You know how much I love magazines.'

'I brought cookies,' he said.

They talked about her treatments, and how soon she would be allowed home.

When she closed her eyes, Danny let her sleep.

He remembered her real hair, and how she tied it up when she came over on hot days to swim in his pool. Jack joined them after work.

One Saturday, there was so much rain that the three of them stayed inside and had too much to drink. They played Monopoly and watched *A Single Man.* Jack smoked a joint and pointed to the television, 'That's like you, Danny, but no one's died.' Danny threw a cushion.

Raquel ordered food from Greenblatt's and they watched *Sixteen Candles.* Jack and Raquel stayed over in a guest bedroom. Danny lay awake, listening to them laugh and move around.

It rained all night.

The next day he called his mother and asked about his dad. She was silent for a while and then told him the whole story, not just the note he taped to the television saying he would never come back – but his childhood in the slums of Manchester, his own father's savage death on a battlefield in northern France. She told him how they met, how he took her out to nice pubs, and picked flowers for her on the viaduct behind their house where steam trains once swished hotly past. The smell of his aftershave. The gentle rough hands from a decade of factory work, and how quickly those hands became fists when anyone called her a name, or made racist remarks.

'I knew deep down he'd go,' she said. 'I was upset, but not surprised.'

She told her son that his father was not the love of her life, just someone she loved along the way.

As Raquel lay sleeping, Danny remembered his life in Scotland, the television studio where it all started and his daily commute through the mouse-grey morning. Then he imagined himself as a child, and felt the small house of his boyhood in Manchester. Cold white bottles on the doorstep, a fish-and-chip shop on the corner run by Bert Echlin, who always gave him an extra sausage. The people *he* had loved along the way.

But there had also been name-calling, insults, people telling him to go back where he came from.

Their words tore into him, because he felt hated, but had done nothing wrong.

People made fun of his neighbour too, an eccentric old man with a deformed head who grew tomatoes and gave them out in small brown bags.

Raquel opened her eyes and blinked a few times. 'How long was I out?'

'Not long, maybe forty minutes.'

'You should have woken me up.'

'Never,' Danny said.

'What did you do while I was asleep?'

'I was remembering this neighbour I had growing up.'

'Your neighbour in Scotland?'

'No, when I was seven or eight. He was the neighbour in Manchester – the city where I was born. He seemed old to me then, but was probably only sixty. His head was deformed, and he spoke with a sort of muted voice. The people on our street called him the elephant man.'

'Jesus, that's unkind.'

Danny nodded. 'I think my mother would remember him, but I hadn't thought of him in years until lately.'

'Tell me more.'

'He grew tomatoes and left them on our doorstep.'

'But you hate tomatoes.'

Danny smiled. 'I also think he taught me to read.'

'Really?' she asked.

'I saw some infomercial in the middle of the night last month and it reminded me of some of the things we did together.'

'An infomercial for what, Danny?'

'Games for kids who are dyslexic.'

'Are you dyslexic?'

Danny looked at her blankly for a few moments. He had always been a slow reader, and remembered the frustration in school when teachers thought he was lazy.

Raquel handed him a tissue.

'Jack and now you,' she said with a smirk. 'What a pair of crybabies.'

Raquel asked if Danny was in contact with this old neighbour.

'He'll have passed away by now, I'm sure,' Danny said. 'And these things always mean more to children, don't they?'

'Look him up,' Raquel said. 'Ask Preston to make some calls.'

Danny shrugged. 'It was all over thirty years ago, and he was pushing sixty then.'

'It won't hurt to try.'

When it was almost time to go, Danny leaned

down and kissed Raquel's head. 'You're so very special, do you know that?'

Somebody passed her room with a trolley.

'If he's alive, he will remember you,' she whispered. 'I guarantee it meant more to him than you think.'

Then a nurse knocked and came in. 'I hope I'm not interrupting.'

'No, not at all,' Danny said. 'I was going to leave soon.'

The nurse checked the machines, and chatted to Raquel about tomorrow's procedures. Danny stood and watched her arrange the sheets. Then she bent down and picked up the empty tote bag.

'Fox Searchlight Pictures,' she said, reading the side of the bag. 'That's my son's dream.'

Raquel leaned forward and the nurse did something to her pillow.

'He's got it in his mind,' she went on, 'that he's going to be the next big thing – a Hollywood director. He's saving up to go to school for it and everything. My husband told him it's not practical. He should study business or computers or something.'

'Danny is a famous film director,' Raquel said brightly.

'Oh?' the nurse asked, adjusting the shades. 'What's your name? I'll tell him I met you.'

When Raquel's face caught a few rays of sunset, Danny saw just how ill she was.

On the way out he stopped in to see the nurse. She was drinking soda with a straw and watching something in Spanish.

'Here's my card,' Danny said. 'Have your son call to set up a meeting at my office.'

'Are you kidding?'

'Just have him call my office.'

She put her soda can down and stood up.

'Oh, mister, is there anything I can do for you? That's so nice of you, I can't believe it. You're going to help my son.'

'Just get her better,' Danny said. 'Just get her better, because without her we're all finished.'

After feeding the dogs, he stayed up and went through boxes of old photographs. A few of the pictures made him cry, because he remembered how it felt to be a child.

After eating a sandwich, he made a list of all the people who had ever loved him. He put it on the refrigerator and read it out loud.

In the morning, he swam in the pool with his dogs, then sat at the kitchen table drawing curved lines. Then he joined those lines and made shapes. The shapes together made words and formed the contents of a letter, which began:

> Dear Mr Hugo,
> You may not remember, but you once saved a child . . .

He drank coffee and read the letter over and over until he knew it by heart.

Then he went outside and sat by the pool.

One of his dogs trotted out and settled at his feet.

He thought of the canal, the piles of litter, the old furniture softened by rain, the weeds in summer, the black water upon which barges once entered and left the city. He saw lorries reversing into the loading bays behind the supermarket. He heard the balcony door slide open and felt the aluminium handle, cold in winter. He remembered his old bedroom in Manchester, the racing-car pyjamas, the squeaky slippers he wore until his toes poked through, his mother's low voice and the lullabies that sailed him off to sleep. Jumping on the bed. Playing cars on the rug. Deciding which teddy to get him through the night.

He stood over the small boy and touched his hair. But the boy did not move – could not feel that he was being remembered.

Danny sat on the bed and traced the outline of cartoon shapes on the duvet. He stared at the plain sleeping face and felt the churn of dreams within.

And then Danny felt a sensation he had never before known, an intense pity that relieved him of an incredible weight. And the boy he reached for in the half dark, the head he touched was not his – but the soft, wispy hair of his sleeping father, as a child, alone, suffering, desperate, and afraid.

AMELIA

EAST SUSSEX, ENGLAND,

2010

I.

MOM MADE SURE Philip was home before she came over to break the news about Grandpa John. Dad was there too, and Dave came later with flowers.

We don't know exactly the moment, but I talked to him the day before and he sounded fine. We spoke for a long time about the new show that was opening with American photographs lost in Europe during World War II.

I told Grandpa John how my job was to make the exhibition accessible to the blind. He wanted to know more, so I explained how one of the photographs was described to me as a young American woman posing on a wall at Coney Island, wearing a dress from Lord & Taylor. I would then find a similar vintage dress for the visitors to feel and smell while explaining to them how the photograph was sent in by Hayley and Sébastien Dazin of St. Pierre, France, after they found it as children in the wreckage of an American B-24 bomber in the woods behind their farm. I told Grandpa John about that photo because he flew in a B-24. I explained how I was going to use the model of the B-24 I had in my room – and boast about how it was the plane that my own grandfather had flown in.

I told him that the museum director loved the name I came up with for the exhibition, and how one of the interns told me she saw a MoMA ad on the side of a New York City bus with the show's name, THE ILLUSION OF SEPARATENESS, in huge letters. I told Grandpa John all this, and he listened and told me how proud he was. I had no idea that it was the last time we would ever speak.

Philip met Grandpa John only once at our wedding in Southampton. They sat talking about the kinds of fish his parents served at the diner growing up.

He wanted to hear Philip's story about how we met, and then couldn't believe it because Harriet proposed to *him* in Montauk near where Philip's boat docks. That's one of the things I loved about Grandpa John – he was always asking questions and trying to make connections.

Philip and I flew to England the day after my parents. Dad picked us up at Heathrow Airport and then drove us to Grandpa John's estate in East Sussex. I was fine on the flight, but when I walked through the front door and could actually smell the house, I realized

Grandpa John had died and we were there to bury his body next to Grandma's.

Dad and Philip went grocery shopping in the afternoon, while Mom and I went through Grandpa's things. She put them in my hands and described them to me. Mom was surprised when I told her to sell the house. It's what she wanted, too, but thought I would have been more upset. Deep down I knew that keeping the house would have become my way of trying to keep Grandpa alive.

'And once it's sold,' I said, 'give the money away – because we're happy as we are, and it's what Grandpa would have wanted.'

'We're talking about millions of pounds, Amelia,' Mom said, but I could tell that part of her agreed.

Then we both cried and held each other. It was a nice moment and helped us prepare for the next few days.

The next day, Philip was exploring and came across Grandpa's old Rolls-Royce, which he used to drive into the village every day for a newspaper and a loaf of bread. It was the only place Grandma had allowed him to smoke cigars. Philip said it needed engine work, but that it was otherwise immaculate. I told Philip that he could have it, but then later on in bed, he said he didn't want it, and I realized how lucky I am to have someone who knows me so well.

A couple of days before the service, Mom took me to her old school. It had closed down and the gates were locked, but we sneaked in. She took me to the place where she used to smoke with the sixth-form girls. Then she drove me to the park where Grandpa took her every Sunday to play on the swings.

Grandpa's nurse discovered him. She said he was on the side of the bed Mrs Bray used to sleep on.

Mom and I stood in his bedroom next to the bed. Then Mom said, 'Oh my God,' and told me how on the bedside table were Grandma's books, her reading glasses, her silver pen, and an empty teacup.

'In his mind, they were still living together,' she said.

And I thought how if Philip died, I wouldn't move his things either.

Over dinner, Mom said it was a miracle Grandpa made it through the war. That he was in a bad way for a long time. Philip asked what happened to him. Mom said that nobody knew the details, but that after being discovered on a battlefield in France, he spent months in a coma at a military hospital. Dad was ripping up newspapers to light a fire and stopped to listen.

Canadian soldiers found him at first light.

Dawn was cool, and the grass wet with night's re-treat. He wasn't wearing any kind of uniform, and walking aimlessly through a field of dead enemy soldiers. When Canadian commandos called out and aimed their rifles, he simply fell over.

They didn't know what to do because he could not be identified. It's lucky that the chief medic considered it his duty to save the young man presented *like a gift from His unseen hand.* After the war, Grandpa and the medic kept in touch. Dr Mohammed went on to become a renowned heart surgeon, and his dream of building a children's cardiac centre in Toronto was eventually realized through an anonymous donor in England.

The flames crackled as we drank wine and laughed about things Grandpa used to say. A few times, I left the room to cry.

Mom got drunk and had to be carried up to bed.

Philip and I stayed downstairs in each other's arms. I could feel the heat on my face like Grandpa watching.

JOHN

FRANCE,

1944

I.

WHEN JOHN WAS about seven years old, he killed a bird.

There was a park near the diner on Long Island, and he used to go there with the other boys to run, shout, and play games. One day someone had a catapult, and they all took turns firing. When it was John's turn to try, he found a small round stone, then placed it in the catapult the way the others had shown him. He closed one eye and took aim at some distant birds in a tree. Nobody could believe it when, from high up in the branches of an old elm, a small body fell to earth.

The other boys patted John on the back and crowded around the lump.

Over dinner that night, John threw up on his plate. As his mother cleaned him off in the bathroom, she noticed his eyes were red from crying. They sat on the couch. John could hardly get the words out.

His father stood quietly and fetched their coats.

He held his hand on the way to the park but they didn't speak. It was cold. People walked their dogs and smoked cigarettes. An old couple out strolling said *good evening* with a smile. The ease of their lives stung sharply.

When they arrived at the park, it was still on the concrete with its legs in the air. They dug at the base of the tree with stones, then John placed the animal in with both hands, and filled the hole.

After several hours, John removed the gun from the enemy soldier's mouth, and rolled off him.

They both had some food, which they shared into a small meal.

Then, without a single word, they stood up and walked away in opposite directions.

John wandered the countryside in a haze for several hours.

Night came again, and the fields around were soon flooded with Allied soldiers. Summer came that night too, and the sky was empty and cool. The stars were crisp, and the planets spun on threads.

It had all been imagined somehow. Harriet, the diner, his sketchbooks, Sunday – not only in name but in feeling. John knew his life had value, because he would die with someone to live for.

He reached for the photograph of Harriet, the one he took at Coney Island. He searched every pocket of his wet, torn clothes, with his eyes barely open, and his body burning hot. But then he remembered taking off from RAF Harrington, and the impact he thought was death, and the smoke, and the freezing descent. Paul and the sticky dolls, the smallest cross, the silent barber and his journey through fields in darkness. His best friend, Leo Arlin, from Brooklyn, the Glen Miller Orchestra, his parents' faces, Lord & Taylor, Harriet proposing to him in Montauk, snow-fall, the sound of cars passing his bedroom window at night. Bare feet. Coney Island in summer.

He could see his wife so clearly now – hear her laugh, even. It was really a fine afternoon. The sub-way cars were full of soldiers. Harriet had to sit on his lap. The weight of her body on his legs was like paradise, and he promised her, in that last great surge of youth, that he would not die unless they were to-gether – even if a picture was the best he could do.

She said that one day they would be very old, that the world would be a different place, but it would always be *their* world, and that the time apart now would be a nightmare from which they would recover – desperation buried under years of happiness.

He groped again for the photograph of his wife, because without it, he could not go on.

AMELIA

EAST SUSSEX, ENGLAND,

2010

I.

GRANDPA'S NURSE SAID he had been acting strangely for a few days, giving her things, asking if she was happy. She said he made her promise to water his plants and feed the hedgehogs that come to the back door at night if anything happened to him.

Mom thinks he knew.

The night before the service I couldn't sleep. Philip tried to stay up with me but fell asleep in his clothes.

In the morning, we went downstairs and made coffee. I didn't say anything, so Philip took me outside for a walk. It was cold and the grass was wet. He led me into a field. The ground was soft, but I could hear something coming towards us and sensed danger. When I asked Philip what it was, he said cows were following at a distance.

When we got back to the house, I felt empty and couldn't stop crying. In the end I didn't know who I was crying for, but it was something my body wanted to do, as though trying to digest grief.

A week later on the flight home, there was severe turbulence. A few people screamed, so the pilot came out to reassure us – which Philip thought was funny.

I thought of Grandpa John parachuting into enemy territory from the fireball of his burning plane. And then all that time in France and then in hospital, not knowing if he was even going to live, not knowing if he would see my grandmother again. Philip said that if he hadn't survived, I wouldn't have been born.

I went to sleep thinking about it. I wondered who would live in our house now if I hadn't been born? I wondered who would have my seat on the bus every day into the city, who would sit next to Philip in his truck on long drives?

One day Philip and I will be old – and this flight home to New York will be a silent flickering, something half imagined. Grandpa John will have been dead for many years.

After Philip and I die, there will be no one left to remember Grandpa John and then no one left to remember us. None of this will have happened, except that it's happening right now.

There will be no Amelia, yet here I am.

I wonder how our bodies will change as we get old. I wonder how we'll feel about things that haven't happened to us yet.

When we get back to our cottage in Sag Harbor,

I'm going to invite all our friends to a summer party, and I'm going to laugh, and put my arms around them. And then I'm going to lead Philip up to bed by the hand, finding the candles by heat, and blowing them out one by one, as we, one day, will be vanquished with a last puff and then nothing at all – nothing but the fragrance of our lives in the world, as on a hand that once held flowers.

MR HUGO

FRANCE,

1944

I.

When a heavy weight suddenly rolled on top of A, panic tore through his body, separating muscle from thought. Then a gun rammed into his mouth. The top of his throat is bleeding. The attacker has clenched teeth. His eyes are wild and bloodshot. Gasping with fear, A is unable to breathe. The barrel digs into his flesh. The taste of blood like old keys.

The other soldiers in his unit had been dead since yesterday afternoon, spread out across the field, dismembered by strafing. They had marched all day with nothing to eat. Then the steady drone of aircraft. A was the only one not running. He anticipated a quick but painful end with brief awareness of shredding. But as the Spitfire pilot dived upon them and they scattered like a flock of clumsy, wingless pigeons, irony tripped A backwards into a tank track, where he remained unconscious long enough for exhaustion to swallow his trembling young frame.

After a period of searing pain, the gun in A's mouth stopped pushing, but remained beyond his teeth. A touched the barrel with his tongue. He wondered if there were any bullets left in the chamber or if his attacker was too injured to fire.

Eventually, A's thoughts drifted to more remote regions. His mother seemed close, even though he had no memory of her face or her voice, or of ever being touched by her hands.

He remembered something from one of her books. He had found a box of them in the attic.

> *If it be not to come, it will be now; if it be not now, yet it will come.*

He was thinking of his mother and her books, and the feel of their pages on his small fingers when the man finally removed the gun from his mouth. A did not move his body. His trousers were soaked with urine, and his lips and mouth cracked with dried blood.

When the man rolled off and slumped down beside him, A reached slowly for his own gun, which he set in the mud beside the other weapon.

He wondered if his attacker was dead. His eyes had closed and he was not moving. He must have been some local Resistant, for he was not in any uniform. Perhaps a farmer driven by the rage of loss.

A touched the man's cheek with the back of his

hand. Then he foraged in his pocket and unwrapped a caramel he had been saving. He pushed it through the man's lips. The eyes did not open, but the jaw turned slowly. His face and neck were like wet sand.

After a few painful chews, the man sat up, but didn't seem to know where he was. A watched as he reached into his pocket and pulled out some dried meat and a bread roll. He dipped the roll in a puddle and broke it in two pieces.

When they finished eating, both men stood up and walked away in opposite directions.

Despite the state of his lips and gums, A stopped from time to time, to pick a blade of grass and balance it in his mouth, the way he used to as a boy.

When he first joined the Hitler Youth, he was presented with a dagger. His father kept taking it down off the mantelpiece to look. He participated in all the programmes because it's what the other boys were doing, and it was nice being in the woods, away from his father, and away from the house. He got through heavy days of training, because the nights were long and full of luxury. Sometimes he lit a candle and read a book.

During one of these weekends, a cabin monitor found a volume of poetry in his pillowcase and reported it. A explained to the chief that his mother had died when he was very young, and in the attic while searching for a compass, he discovered a chest of her things. The book was returned to him, but the other boys turned against him after that. One told him that young men should lift weights and wrestle.

One afternoon when his father was out, A found another book. It was a slim volume with sentences that flowed from his mouth like warm water.

A slept under a tree the first night. It was humid and the sky was overcast. In the morning he opened his eyes and lay without moving. There were birds everywhere. He need only be killed and it would be over.

He might even see his mother. But how would he explain the things he had let himself do?

He bent back thorny branches to find berries growing in the hedgerows.

He measured distance by his position to the sun.

For two days he walked in circles, then hunger compelled him east, where he imagined other Nazi divisions were digging in. He would be fed and looked after. There would have to be a report. At first he would not be without blame, not without suspicion. Then a fresh uniform and a place to sleep.

Imagining all this, A longed for another chance to be cut down by some low-flying Englishman in a fast plane. He should have given up earlier. He should have buried his dagger in the garden to go blunt. He had heard about the others, those in his village who disagreed, or thought Hitler was mad, or sympathized with the condemned. They quickly disappeared, leaving their families to continue on without them in disgrace and longing.

And when the war started, there was gossip it would end early with concessions and treaties and brass bands. But it did not, and he was soon part of a convoy headed for France. The older troops who fought in the first war told them it would be a battle with the French to the death. But then the vicious army they imagined did not appear, or they were in the wrong place, and it would come later.

There *were* attacks, but they were isolated and unorganized. A's first kill was a figure shooting at him from across a river. And then a boy his own age at close range whose throat opened like a pair of wings.

He did what they told him to do. He would have done anything they told him to do. He hid inside the pronoun *we*.

In the afternoon, a squadron of bombers flew over at low altitude and dropped their load several kilometres ahead. Distant thunder. Silent plumes of crow-black smoke.

A continued over the fields, his muddied jacket under one arm as though out for a country stroll.

One kilometre or so later, A came upon a barn on fire. The earth was dug out in places and there was splintered wood.

On the ground were the charred remains of a woman still holding a bucket. The flames crackled and tore at the afternoon. A sat where he could feel the heat of the burning wood.

When the wind changed, an edge of the farmhouse roof caught fire. A had been thinking how he might stay there for a few days, but the whole house would soon be engulfed. At the last minute A realized that there might be food inside, and hurried towards the kitchen door.

It was cool and shady. There were stone floors and heavy plates in a line on a shelf. The plates were light brown with thin cracks that made them seem old, like faces with nothing to say and nothing to see. One smaller plate had rabbits painted on it. The rabbits were in top hats. An inscription on the plate said:

Le Lièvre: Il y a souvent plus de courage à fuir qu'à combattre.

A once had a pet rabbit. It was called Felix and used to follow him around in the fields beyond the cottage. A used to lie on his back and Felix would sniff him and A would giggle. One night over dinner, A's father couldn't stop laughing. After watching his son eat a second helping of stew, he told him to go check on Felix.

Sunlight reached in through the farmhouse window with arms of smoke. On the table was a knife and squares of fabric cut into rectangles. There were also large safety pins, which glinted in the sunlight.

After a quick search, A found three onions in a basket and a few sticks of old celery. There was also a jug of milk with an inch of cream at the top. A cradled everything into his arms and was about to leave when he glanced at the rabbit plate and considered how it would feel to have a book, any book, even one in French that he would not fully understand. He dumped everything outside and ran upstairs.

The landing was thick with smoke and A had to hold his breath. In the first room was a pair of narrow beds with two white blankets, frayed but pulled neatly over pillows. There were two bedside tables of dark wood, a square clock, and a wooden closet with mirrors set in the doors.

A rushed to the window and flung it open. He filled his lungs with clean air, as smoke poured out over his shoulders. From the second floor he could see the body of the woman more clearly. The heat from the burning roof was intense.

A went back into the room and scooped out an armful of men's clothes that were hanging in the closet. He tossed them through the open window and watched them flutter to the ground.

In the second room was a chest of drawers and, to A's utter delight, a small stack of books. There was little time to choose, so A grabbed the thickest volume, which he then dropped in his excitement. As he bent down to pick it up, he noticed at the far end of the room a mess of blankets and a makeshift cot from which a round face was blinking furiously.

II.

A SET THE screaming child down by the cow fence and covered the body of the woman with his jacket. He changed out of his ruined uniform and dressed in the shirt, trousers, and jacket from upstairs. Then the baby stopped crying and watched A roll his old clothes into a ball and toss them into the fire.

There was a cattle trough by the fence, brimming with rainwater. Insects skimmed along the top. Dead slugs had turned white and rolled at the bottom. A splashed the mud and smoke off his face, then brushed back his hair with both hands.

When the baby started crying again, A fetched the jug of milk and put some cream on his finger. The child took it eagerly then reached for more. A tried many positions, but not one of them seemed appropriate for feeding. He had never witnessed a child fed by a mother before, nor felt the warmth of another human body against his. The child, being turned sideways, and spun, and held upside down by A, thought it was a game, and his crying turned to laughter.

In the end, A poured milk into the palm of his hand and the child licked it out. After a dozen palmfuls, the child looked up and made a noise that sounded like *meow*.

They sat there for a long time deciding what to do.

The child kept looking around. A knew why, and it filled him with despair.

At the edge of the farm was a gate. A few birds had perched to watch the flames. A imagined another child waiting at another gate for his father, and recalled vividly the forms and faces of those men he had cut down.

And through all this, the child clung to him, and A clung to the child.

They had a long way to go.

This would be the first day.

III.

HIS FATHER WOULD think he had been killed. He could read books again, sit in fields, fall asleep outside, and go back to the secret rural life he so enjoyed. He could raise the child as his own son, teach him to read and write. They would take all their meals together, make each other laugh, grow things in a small garden, and go swimming in summer, when the rivers were shallow.

His mother seemed to him now more alive than she ever had – as though he were taking over from her somehow and the child in his arms was himself.

He knew that people would be suspicious of a

young man who didn't speak – but he had a baby. He was carrying a person too young to know about war.

Slow convoys of German soldiers eyed A and the child with indifference. French peasantry who, on getting little response to their questions, threw their hands in the air or hurled insults that A did not understand. After a few days, they were both desperately hungry, and the child wouldn't stop crying. If not for an old woman who noticed a man and baby stumbling along the road – it might have ended for both of them quite soon.

Her first task was to feed the child, but just enough to begin the process of eating again.

The woman had a skeletal face with deep-set, serious eyes that gave the appearance of chronic disapproval. She arranged her grey hair meticulously, in the style of a bourgeois. A thought that at one time she had probably been quite beautiful. He wondered if she had any children, and where they were. A dry mop stood upside down in the corner of her sitting room like someone watching, and beside the fire there were two wooden armchairs, one of which appeared unused. There were sheets of newspaper on the floor, and from time to time, a cat wandered past with its tail up.

A's silence did not seem to bother the woman. She

had lived alone for a long time and was not used to speaking. Her initial fear was that the man would beat her. But after a few hours, her fear was that they would leave.

A sipped hot broth before a crackling fire, and watched the old woman lay the baby on a towel, then unpin the soiled cloth around its bottom. She wiped gently with a warm rag and the child screamed. She rinsed out the rag and continued wiping. The flesh on the child's genitals and upper legs was raw. The child was screaming with such force that his face had turned blue. A put down the bowl of broth and went to him.

When the child saw A, he calmed a little and his screaming turned to crying. After several shallow breaths, he fell silent and reached out his hands. A touched them. The woman smiled and applied a white paste to the baby's raw skin with her fingers.

The next day she cut up one of her old dresses and showed A how to pin a piece of fabric safely onto the child.

After they had eaten supper that night, she demonstrated how to hold the baby against his shoulder, and pat the middle of his back.

In a trunk upstairs, the woman found A a pair of shoes, which were too big, but cushioned his ruined feet as they foraged each night in the dusk for potatoes, turnips, carrots, or anything remotely edible. Whatever they unearthed was first offered to the child.

One day a man knocked on the door. When the woman opened it and spoke to him, he said he was lost, but couldn't stop looking at A, who stood behind with the baby. The next day, two men kept walking past the house and trying to look in. When gunshots were heard in a nearby field that evening, A decided they would leave at dawn.

The woman filled a basket with clean rags, apples, and anything else she had lying around.

She stood in the middle of the road and watched them disappear.

That night in bed she held her rosary and wondered who else she could help.

On her deathbed thirty-eight years later in 1982, still clutching her rosary, the old woman felt the measure of her loss through the grief of those at her bedside. She tried to appear calm but was in a great deal of pain. She was known simply as Marie, though older people liked to call her Mairie,* to show their respect for all she had done for people over the years.

When the moon came out, she exhaled a final

* Town council.

breath and the most insignificant part of her slipped away with grace.

The entire village took part in the funeral procession. Behind the hearse, the priest talked loudly and laughed because she had taught him the joy not only in life. Teenagers followed slowly at the back, keeping distance enough to smoke and hold hands.

IV.

A AND THE CHILD slept mostly in barns. When it rained, they found shelter under thick summer trees. If there was no one around, A read to the child from the book in his pocket. And though neither of them understood what the words meant, the sound of it gave them peace.

A knew how to harvest the wild hedgerows, and the child soon developed a taste for blueberries and strawberries. They found a rhythm for eating and sleeping, and the child seemed content – except at night, when he often woke and was inconsolable.

A changed his nappy always in the morning,

at noon, and in the evening. If not too soiled, he would keep the old pieces to wash later. He also applied the white paste given to him in a jar by the old woman.

There were a few times when the child was screaming so much that A got worried, and so broke his silence and hummed the only song he loved, that he had heard as a child, and which haunted him with mysterious familiarity. He liked to think of it as something his mother had taught him. He did not know who wrote it, when, or why – that it was called *Of Foreign Lands and People*, and that his mother had received a standing ovation when she played it to a packed school auditorium in 1911.

One morning, they found a bicycle in some damp hay. With a little practise, A figured out a way to keep it going with both of them on.

After hours gliding through the countryside, they approached a village so small there wasn't even a sign. In the distance outside a café, a group of Nazi soldiers were standing in the road, smoking and talking. The child could feel A's fear and clung tightly. In a flash of inspiration, A rang the bell on the handlebars and the soldiers instinctively separated to let them pass through the middle.

By noon the next day there were gradually more buildings, more people, and a steady stream of sputtering cars with things strapped to the roof.

When they saw the Eiffel Tower in the distance, A got off the bicycle and wheeled it. They had no more food and the baby was restless. Eventually, it was too much for A to bear, and so, holding the child in his arms, he stepped into the first café that looked friendly. A man in a short brown tie greeted him. A tried to convey, using his hands, that he wanted to sell the bicycle outside, or trade it for something to eat.

People stopped eating and looked. The owner held meal tickets to A's face and shrugged. Then a waiter began to usher them out, wrinkling his nose in disgust at the smell of the child. When they were almost to the door, an elegant woman in a red dress strode over to the owner and slapped him hard on the cheek. Then a chair scraped because an old man at the back of the dining room had stood up to see.

The woman took the baby from A's arms and went back to her table, where she mashed her lunch into tiny morsels. A few people applauded. Others shook their heads in disgust.

A stood by the door and watched the boy reach madly for the food on the woman's plate. He felt giddy with delight. The waiter went back to work.

As people finished their meals and left the restaurant, some handed A a piece of cheese, or bread, or meat wrapped in newspaper. One woman told him he should be ashamed of himself, begging like that with a child.

Before giving the baby back to A, the elegant woman wrote her name on a piece of paper, along with her address in the Ninth Arrondissement. Then she kissed the child and walked out.

They wandered the boulevards of Paris for hours like a pair of tourists. A's feet ached in a new way. He wanted to tell the baby that Paris was like a poem in stone. He thought about the woman in the red dress, and wondered if they would live with her from now on. She was very attractive, and in time, they might even grow to love one another. He could get a job, fix up her place – read to them at night for entertainment.

They came upon the Louvre Palace by accident, and ambled through an archway into the Tuileries, where A set down the bicycle and found a sunny patch of grass.

They played, clapped hands, and rolled in the grass. Bees shouldered their way into soft bells, and birds circled noiselessly above the fountains. When A took a small, plump tomato from his pocket, the child snatched it, but instead of eating it, held it to A's lips.

He bounced the boy on his lap, and from time to time, fed him pieces of food from his pocket. Old people stopped walking to look at them.

A collected fallen petals from the flower beds and rained them down over the child. The statues seemed to protect them without moving.

When the baby cried, A hummed quietly and cradled him.

They fell asleep with their foreheads touching.

When other people began to pack up and go, A looked for the woman's address in his pocket, and set the child on the bicycle. The sun was beginning to set, and night would be cool.

When they reached a wide square of cobblestones at the edge of the Tuileries, A noticed people congregating on the rue de Rivoli, and thought it might be a good place to get directions. He would show the piece of paper with the address, then point questioningly.

At the centre of the crowd was a stout old man with a small dog that was doing tricks. A leaned the bicycle against a wall, and pushed to the front so the baby could see. The dog was wearing a tiny beret and a tricolour coat. People applauded when he stood on his back legs. The old man was delighted and blushed.

After a short time, the crowd had grown so large that pedestrians had to step into the road to pass. There was no end to the dog's folly. A wondered if they were once part of a circus. When the crowd laughed, A and the child laughed with them.

Then angry shouting in a language that A understood. People strained their necks to see what was happening. The crowd was so large that a motorcycle and sidecar were unable to turn up a narrow street. The driver shouted in French, then in German, but the dog had put everyone in a trance.

The soldier climbed out of the sidecar and muscled his way through the crowd. He shouted at the man to take his animal and clear off.

The man made a face and turned to his little dog. The soldier shook his head in reproach and pointed for the man to go. Then the little dog shook his head and raised a paw in the same direction.

The crowd screamed with laughter.

A and the baby laughed too because the dog had done it without any sign from his master. The soldier pushed the old man to the ground. The crowd surged and shouted viciously. When the dog attacked the soldier's ankle, he pinned his body with his boot and drove the butt of his rifle hard upon the dog's skull, dashing it against the stone. The crowd broke into violent screams, and rushed upon the soldier. A felt in danger of being crushed but couldn't get away. The soldier, cornered by the fierce mob, waved his gun frantically back and forth.

Then gendarmes arrived blowing whistles. They tried to break up the crowd, but people were resisting. A wrapped the child safely in his arms and tried to shoulder their way out of the mayhem, but then nudged a gendarme in the back who quickly turned around and demanded to see his identity papers. A tried to back away slowly, but the policeman raised his pistol and demanded identification.

' "I have no way," ' A said in English, ' "and therefore want no eyes; I stumbled when I saw." '

There was a moment of connection, which may only have been confusion, but the gendarme's father had been an English teacher in Le Mans and often recited lines from Shakespeare at the dinner table on Sunday.

Then military vehicles arrived. Soldiers beat anyone in their way.

One of the soldiers must have thought that A was resisting arrest, and stormed past the gendarme with his rifle out. The policeman told the soldier to lower his gun, but his eyes were burning. A quickly handed the child to a teenage girl standing next to him, and raised his arms in surrender. The soldier pushed the barrel of his rifle against A's forehead and screamed. Then some of the other soldiers began firing and the crowd went mad. As the soldier prepared to fire upon A, the teenage girl, still holding the child, realized that she was looking at the same soldier who had killed her brother last year outside a café as she and her mother watched helplessly. Without hesitation, she took a pistol from her pocket and shot the soldier twice in the heart. A gendarme several yards away fired at the girl, but missed and hit A in the face. People found themselves spotted with blood and fragments of bone.

The teenage girl dropped the gun and ran, still holding the baby in her arms. A team of soldiers gave chase, but Anne-Lise was a fast runner. She grew up in a village outside Paris and was a champion ice-skater.

She had taken part in many missions under the name Sainte Anne. She had killed nine people and always cried after – but would never give up. She was seventeen years old, and her heart was a determined one.

In her pocket were keys, a small notebook of poems, a pencil stub, some string, and a ring her mother had given her for her thirteenth birthday.

She had been asked to leave Paris for a while by

the others because she was known to the enemy – but news of the Normandy landings had reached the city. The liberation was a matter of weeks. Plans were being concocted, weapons smuggled in. Sainte Anne's skills and daring would be vital.

She sprinted towards the river, stumbling on loose cobbles, but never losing her balance. Her hope was to get ahead and then hide under a bridge, or in a boat moored to the bank.

Other moments of her life passed as she darted across streets, through trees, down ancient stone steps.

The smell of oil on her father's hands. The night she left the window open at her grandparents' house and snow settled on her bedclothes. Riding a horse for a bet and then falling in love. Lacing up her ice skates. She wanted to marry and live in Montmartre. She loved dancing and American jazz.

As she hurried down the steps to the river, she looked up to see the soldiers passing above. She slowed and tried to appear calm – but then someone sitting idly by the water whistled, and the soldiers turned around.

As she flew up a narrow bank of the Seine, the soldiers shouted at her to stop. They were closing in and the child in her arms was a terrible, screaming weight.

After passing under another bridge, she spotted a

narrow staircase that led back to the street. The soldiers followed her up the steps one by one. When she reached a long, straight boulevard, two of the soldiers stopped to fire. Someone screamed. People on bicycles pedalled for their lives. Anne-Lise saw an alley and cut into it, but then halfway down realized it was a dead end.

These were to be the last moments of their lives.

But then a door swung open and a surprised teenage boy in a baker's apron stood looking at her. She pushed past him into the storeroom and told him to close the door quickly.

It was very dark. They could hear the soldiers' boots outside. Then the sound of rifle butts slammed against doors and the order to open up. When the baby started to cry, they bashed at the baker's door, and kicked it with their boots.

Pascal took the baby from Anne-Lise and told her to stay hidden under a pile of sacks.

Then he unbolted the door with the child in his arms.

The soldiers stared at them angrily.

'What's going on?' Pascal said. 'What do you want?'

'Who else is in there?' one of them growled.

'My mother is sleeping upstairs.'

'What about your wife?'

'She went to visit her grandfather in Tours, who says he's dying but probably has the flu,' Pascal said. 'This is my son.'

'Your son?' one of the soldiers said. 'What's his name?'

'Martin,' Pascal said.

The soldiers stared menacingly until Pascal asked if they would like to come in for some hot coffee and something to eat. They entered without saying anything and walked through the kitchen into the place where there were tables. They took off their helmets and set them noisily on the floor. The shop had just closed, but Pascal put on all the lights and warmed some cakes in the oven, as if it were just another, ordinary day.

ACKNOWLEDGEMENTS

The author would like to mention how the story of John and Harriet Bray is inspired, in part, by the real-life story of Bert and Annette Knapp. During World War II, Mr Knapp served in the Eighth Air Force and was a recipient of the Distinguished Flying Cross and the Purple Heart. He was a member of Operation Carpetbagger when his B-24 Liberator crashed in Nazi-occupied France on 7 August 1944, after being hit by flak. He died in 1994. Mrs Knapp is ninety-four years old and lives in Connecticut.

The author wishes to acknowledge the following:

Amy Baker; the O'Brien family; Joshua Bodwell; Bryan Le Boeuf; BookCourt; Dr A. S. and Mrs J. E. Booy; my dear brother Darren Booy and his wife, Raha; Catrin Brace and the Welsh Assembly Government; Ken Browar; David Bruson; Jonathan Burnham; Gabriel Byrne; Lauren Cerand; the Connelly family; Mary Beth Constant; Rejean Daigneault; Dr Shilpi Epstein; Laurie Fink; Peggy Flaum; Tom Ford; Foxy; the Gaddis family; Dr Bruce Gelb; Rich Green; Jen Hart; Dr Maryhelen Hendricks at SVA; Dolores

Henry; Gregory Henry; Nancy Horner; Mr Howard; Carrie Howland; Dr M. Kempner; Alan Kleinberg; Hilary Knight; Babette Kulik; the Lotos Club; Alain Malraux; Lisa Mamo; Michael and Delphine Matkin; McNally Jackson Booksellers; Dr Edmund Miller; Dr Bob Milgrom at SVA; Cal Morgan; Michael Morrison; Dr William Neal of Campbellsville University; Neil Olson; Orchard Strategies; Wendy and Jon Paton; Lukas Ortiz; Deborah Ory; Jonathan D. Rabinowitz; Rob; *Shambhala Sun* magazine; Ivan Shaw and Lisa Von Weise Shaw; Society Club; Dmitri Shostakovich; Philip G. Spitzer; Vi Trayte; the Vilcek Foundation; Virginia Stanley; Jeremy Strong; Lorilee Van Booy; Fred Volkmer; Dr Barbara Wersba; Sylvia Beach Whitman at Shakespeare & Company.

Also:

Jean-Pierre Melville for *L'Armée des Ombres* (Army of Shadows), a scene from which served as the inspiration for John Bray's interaction with the barber.

The inscription on John Bray's gravestone was written by P. S. Moffat, and taught to me by my daughter.

For their selflessness, attention to detail, and dedication, the author would like to recognize the following individuals and staff:

Serge Blandin; Thomas Ensminger; Colonel Robert Fish for *They Flew by Night*; United States Holocaust Memorial Museum; the Imperial War Museum, London; the Jewish Museum; the Metropolitan Museum of Art; MoMA; Musée de la Résistance Nationale; the Parrish Art Museum, Southampton; Roy Tebbutt, Fred West, and Keith Taylor of the Carpetbagger Aviation Museum at Harrington; Pierre Tillet.

And very special thanks to:

My partner, Christina Daigneault, for her love, kindness, profound intelligence, support, discreet notes, and Bach duets;

Lucas Hunt, poet, confidant, best friend;

Enormous thanks, as always, to Carrie Kania, my guiding light, whose friendship, confidence, editorial insight, style, and devotion made this book possible:

Michael Signorelli, my kind, charismatic, and deeply intelligent editor;

Madeleine Van Booy, the most wonderful, brilliant, and talented daughter a father could ever wish for.

The team at Conville and Walsh:

Jake Smith-Bosanquet, Alexandra McNicoll, and Henna Silvennoinen, for their remarkable talents, kindness, and outstanding achievements on behalf of their authors.

ABOUT THE AUTHOR

SIMON VAN BOOY is the author of two novels and two collections of short stories, including *The Secret Lives of People in Love* and *Love Begins in Winter*, which won the Frank O'Connor International Short Story Award. He is the editor of three philosophy books and has written for the *New York Times*, the *Guardian*, NPR, and the BBC. His work has been translated into fifteen languages. He lives in Brooklyn with his wife and daughter.

www.SimonVanBooy.com